THE FAMILY READ-ALOUD

CHRISTMAS
TREASURY

THE FAMILY READ-ALOUD
CHRISTMAS TREASURY

SELECTED BY ALICE LOW
ILLUSTRATED BY MARC BROWN

A TRUMPET CLUB SPECIAL EDITION

For Roger and Ann, with love
—A.L.

For Grandma Thora
Thank you for making my early Christmases
so memorable
—M.B.

Published by The Trumpet Club
1540 Broadway, New York, New York 10036

Text selection copyright © 1989 by Alice Low
Illustrations copyright © 1989 by Marc Brown

ISBN 0-440-84448-7

This edition published by arrangement with Joy Street/Little, Brown and Company (Inc.)

Acknowledgments begin on page 133.

Book design by Sylvia Frezzolini
Printed in the United States of America
November 1991

10 9 8 7 6 5 4 3 2
KP

CONTENTS

THE FAMILY READ-ALOUD

CHRISTMAS
TREASURY

IN THE WEEK WHEN CHRISTMAS COMES

This is the week when Christmas comes.

Let every pudding burst with plums,
And every tree bear dolls and drums,
    In the week when Christmas comes.

Let every hall have boughs of green,
With berries glowing in between,
    In the week when Christmas comes.

Let every doorstep have a song
Sounding the dark street along,
    In the week when Christmas comes.

Let every steeple ring a bell
With a joyful tale to tell,
    In the week when Christmas comes.

Let every night put forth a star
To show us where the heavens are,
    In the week when Christmas comes.

Let every stable have a lamb
Sleeping warm beside its dam,
    In the week when Christmas comes.

This is the week when Christmas comes.

ELEANOR FARJEON

CHRISTMAS IS COMING

Christmas is coming,
The geese are getting fat,
Please put a penny
In the old man's hat.
If you haven't got a penny,
A ha'penny will do;
If you haven't got a ha'penny,
Then God bless you!

ENGLISH RHYME

DAY BEFORE CHRISTMAS

We have been helping with the cake
  And licking out the pan,
And wrapping up our packages
  As neatly as we can.
And we have hung our stockings up
  Beside the open grate,
And now there's nothing more to do
  Except
    To
      Wait!

MARCHETTE CHUTE

DECEMBER

First snow! The flakes
   So few, so light,
Remake the world
   In solid white.

All bundled up,
   We feel as if
We were fat penguins,
   Warm and stiff.

Downtown, the stores
   Half split their sides,
And Mother brings home
   Things she hides.

Old carols peal.
   The dusk is dense.
There is a mood
   Of sweet suspense.

The shepherds wait,
   The kings, the tree—
All wait for something
   Yet to be,

Some miracle.
   And then it's here,
Wrapped up in hope—
   Another year!

JOHN UPDIKE

DIMMEST AND BRIGHTEST MONTH AM I

Dimmest and brightest month am I;
  My short days end, my lengthening days
    begin;
What matters more or less sun in the sky,
  When all is sun within?

CHRISTINA ROSSETTI

RAMONA AND THE THREE WISE PERSONS

BEVERLY CLEARY

Suddenly, a few days before Christmas when the Quimby family least expected it, the telephone rang for Ramona's father. He had a job! The morning after New Year's Day he was to report for training as a checker in a chain of supermarkets. The pay was good, he would have to work some evenings, and maybe someday he would get to manage a market!

After that telephone call Mr. Quimby stopped reaching for cigarettes that were not there and began to whistle as he ran the vacuum cleaner and folded the clothes from the dryer. The worried frown disappeared from Mrs. Quimby's forehead. Beezus looked even more calm and serene. Ramona, however, made a mistake. She told her mother about her tight shoes. Mrs. Quimby then wasted a Saturday afternoon shopping for shoes when she could have been sewing on Ramona's costume for the Christmas pageant. As a result, when they drove to church the night of the Christmas program, Ramona was the only unhappy member of the family.

Mrs. Quimby leaned back, tired but relaxed. Beezus smiled her gentle Virgin Mary pageant smile that Ramona had found so annoying for the past three weeks.

Ramona sulked.

Mr. Quimby sang, "Oh, I feel like shouting in my heart. . . ."

Ramona interrupted her father's song. "I don't care what anybody says," she burst out. "If I can't be a good sheep, I am not going to be a sheep at all." She yanked off the white terry-cloth headdress with pink-lined ears that she was wearing and stuffed it into the pocket of her car coat. She started to pull her father's rolled-down socks from her hands because they didn't really look like hooves, but then she decided they kept her hands warm. She squirmed on the lumpy terry-cloth tail sewn to the seat of her pajamas. Ramona could not pretend that faded pajamas printed with an army of pink rabbits, half of them upside down, made her look like a sheep, and Ramona was usually good at pretending.

Mrs. Quimby's voice was tired. "Ramona, your tail and headdress were all I could manage, and I had to stay up late last night to finish those. I simply don't have time for complicated sewing."

Ramona knew that. Her family had been telling her so for the past three weeks.

"A sheep should be woolly," said Ramona. "A sheep should not be printed with pink bunnies."

"You can be a sheep that has been shorn," said Mr. Quimby, who was full of jokes now that he was going to work again. "Or how about a wolf in sheep's clothing?"

"You just want me to be miserable," said Ramona, not appreciating her father's humor and feeling that everyone in her family should be miserable because she was.

"She's worn out," said Mrs. Quimby, as if Ramona could not hear. "It's so hard to wait for Christmas at her age."

Ramona raised her voice. "I am *not* worn out! You know sheep don't wear pajamas."

"That's show biz," said Mr. Quimby.

"Daddy!" Beezus-Mary was shocked. "It's church!"

The sight of light shining through the stained-glass window of the big stone church diverted Ramona for a moment. The window looked beautiful, as if it were made of jewels.

Mr. Quimby backed the car into a parking space. "Ho-ho-ho!" he said as he turned off the ignition. "'Tis the season to be jolly."

Jolly was the last thing Ramona was going to be. Leaving the car, she stooped down inside her car coat to hide as many rabbits as possible. Black branches clawed at the rain-filled sky, and the wind was raw.

"Stand up straight," said Ramona's heartless father.

"I'll get wet," said Ramona. "I might catch cold, and then you'd be sorry."

"Run between the drops," said Mr. Quimby.

"They're too close together," answered Ramona.

"Oh, you two," said Mrs. Quimby with a tired little laugh as she backed out of the car and tried to open her umbrella at the same time.

"I will not be in it," Ramona defied her family once and for all. "They can give the program without me."

Her father's answer was a surprise. "Suit yourself," he said. "You're not going to spoil our evening."

Mrs. Quimby gave the seat of Ramona's pajamas an affectionate pat. "Run along, little lamb, wagging your tail behind you."

Ramona walked stiff-legged so that her tail would not wag.

At the church door the family parted, the girls going downstairs to the Sunday-school room, which was a confusion of chattering children piling coats and raincoats on chairs. Ramona found a corner

behind the Christmas tree, where Santa would pass out candy canes after the program. She sat down on the floor with her car coat pulled over her bent knees.

Nobody noticed Ramona. Everyone was having too much fun. Shepherds found their cloaks, which were made from old cotton bedspreads. Beezus's friend, Henry Huggins, arrived and put on the dark robe he was to wear in the part of Joseph.

The other two sheep appeared. Howie's acrylic sheep suit, with the zipper on the front, was as thick and as fluffy as Ramona knew it would be. Ramona longed to pet Howie; he looked so soft. Davy's flannel suit was fastened with safety pins, and there was something wrong about the ears. If his tail had been longer, he could have passed for a kitten, but he did not seem to mind. Both boys wore brown mittens. Davy, who was a thin little sheep, jumped up and down to make his tail wag, which surprised Ramona. At school he was always so shy. Maybe he felt brave inside his sheep suit. Howie, a chunky sheep, made his tail wag, too. My ears are as good as theirs, Ramona told herself. The floor felt cold through the seat of her thin pajamas.

"Look at the little lambs!" cried an angel. "Aren't they darling?"

"Ba-a, ba-a!" bleated Davy and Howie.

Ramona longed to be there with them, jumping and ba-a-ing and wagging her tail, too. Maybe the faded rabbits didn't show as much as she had thought. She sat hunched and miserable. She had told her father she would *not* be a sheep, and she couldn't back down now. She hoped God was too busy to notice her, and then she changed her mind. Please, God, prayed Ramona, in case He wasn't too busy to listen to a miserable little sheep, I don't really mean to be horrid. It just works out that way. She was frightened, she discovered, for when the program began, she would be left alone in the church basement. The lights might even be turned out, a scary thought, for the big stone church filled Ramona with awe, and she did not want to be left alone in the dark with her awe. Please, God, prayed Ramona, get me out of this mess.

Beezus, in a long blue robe with a white scarf over her head and carrying a baby's blanket and a big flashlight, found her little sister. "Come out, Ramona," she coaxed. "Nobody will notice your costume. You know Mother would have made you a whole sheep suit if she had time. Be a good sport. Please."

Ramona shook her head and blinked to keep tears from falling. "I told Daddy I wouldn't be in the program, and I won't."

"Well, okay, if that's the way you feel," said Beezus, forgetting to act like Mary. She left her little sister to her misery.

Ramona sniffed and wiped her eyes on her hoof. Why didn't some grown-up come along and *make* her join the other sheep? No grown-up came. No one seemed to remember there were supposed to be three sheep, not even Howie, who played with her almost every day.

Ramona's eye caught the reflection of her face distorted in a green Christmas ornament. She was shocked to see her nose look huge, her mouth and red-rimmed eyes tiny. I can't really look like that, thought Ramona in despair. I'm really a nice person. It's just that nobody understands.

Ramona mopped her eyes on her hoof again, and as she did she noticed three big girls, so tall they were probably in the eighth grade, putting on robes made from better bedspreads than the shepherd's robes. That's funny, she thought. Nothing she had learned in Sunday

school told her anything about girls in long robes in the Nativity scene. Could they be Jesus's aunts?

One of the girls began to dab tan cream from a little jar on her face and to smear it around while another girl held up a pocket mirror. The third girl, holding her own mirror, used an eyebrow pencil to give herself heavy brows.

Makeup, thought Ramona with interest, wishing she could wear it. The girls took turns darkening their faces and brows. They looked like different people.

One of the girls noticed her. "Hi, there," she said. "Why are you hiding back there?"

"Because," was Ramona's all-purpose answer. "Are you Jesus's aunts?" she asked.

The girls found the question funny. "No," answered one. "We're the Three Wise Persons."

Ramona was puzzled. "I thought they were supposed to be wise *men*," she said.

"The boys backed out at the last minute," explained the girl with the blackest eyebrows. "Mrs. Russo said women can be wise, too, so tonight we are the Three Wise Persons."

This idea seemed like a good one to Ramona, who wished she were big enough to be a wise person hiding behind makeup so nobody would know who she was.

"Are you supposed to be in the program?" asked one of the girls.

"I was supposed to be a sheep, but I changed my mind," said Ramona, changing it back again. She pulled out her sheep headdress and put it on.

"Isn't she adorable?" said one of the wise persons.

Ramona was surprised. She had never been called adorable before. Bright, lively, yes; adorable, no. She smiled and felt more lovable. Maybe pink-lined ears helped.

"Why don't you want to be a sheep?" asked a wise person.

Ramona had an inspiration. "Because I don't have any makeup."

"Makeup on a *sheep*!" exclaimed a wise person, and giggled.

Ramona persisted. "Sheep have black noses," she hinted. "Maybe I could have a black nose."

The girls looked at one another. "Don't tell my mother," said one, "but I have some mascara. We could make her nose black."

"Please!" begged Ramona, getting to her feet and coming out from behind the Christmas tree.

The owner of the mascara fumbled in her shoulder bag, which was hanging on a chair, and brought out a tiny box. "Let's go in the kitchen where there's a sink," she said, and when Ramona followed her, she moistened an elf-sized brush, which she rubbed on the mascara in the box. Then she began to brush it onto Ramona's nose. It tickled, but Ramona held still. "It feels like brushing my teeth only on my nose," she remarked. The wise person stood back to look at her work and then applied another coat of mascara to Ramona's nose. "There," she said at last. "Now you look like a real sheep."

Ramona felt like a real sheep. "Ba-a-a," she bleated, a sheep's way of saying thank you. Ramona felt so much better, she could almost pretend she was woolly. She peeled off her coat and found that the faded pink rabbits really didn't show much in the dim light. She pranced off among the angels, who had been handed little flashlights, which they were supposed to hold like candles. Instead they were shining them into their mouths to show one another how weird they looked with light showing through their cheeks. The other two sheep stopped jumping when they saw her.

"You don't look like Ramona," said Howie.

"B-a-a. I'm not Ramona. I'm a sheep." The boys did not say one word about Ramona's pajamas. They wanted black noses too, and when Ramona told them where she got hers, they ran off to find the wise persons. When they returned, they no longer looked like Howie and Davy in sheep suits. They looked like strangers in sheep suits. So I must really look like somebody else, thought Ramona with increasing happiness. Now she could be in the program, and her parents wouldn't know because they wouldn't recognize her.

"B-a-a!" bleated three prancing, black-nosed sheep. "B-a-a, b-a-a."

Mrs. Russo clapped her hands. "Quiet, everybody!" she ordered. "All right, Mary and Joseph, up by the front stairs. Shepherds and sheep next and then wise persons. Angels line up by the back stairs."

Ramona's heart began to pound as if something exciting were about to happen. Up the stairs she tiptoed and through the arched door. The only light came from candelabra on either side of the chancel and from a streetlight shining through a stained-glass window. Ramona had never seen the church look so beautiful or so mysterious.

Beezus sat down on a low stool in the center of the chancel and arranged the baby's blanket around the flashlight. Henry stood behind her. The sheep got down on their hands and knees in front of the shepherds, and the Three Wise Persons stood off to one side, holding bath-salts jars that looked as if they really could hold frankincense and myrrh.

A shivery feeling ran down Ramona's backbone, as if magic were taking place. She looked up at Beezus, smiling tenderly down at the flashlight, and it seemed as if Baby Jesus really could be inside the blanket.

Then Ramona found her parents in the second row. They were smiling gently, proud of Beezus. This gave Ramona an aching feeling inside. They would not know her in her makeup. Maybe they would think she was some other sheep, and she didn't want to be some other sheep. She wanted to be their sheep. She wanted them to be proud of her, too.

Ramona saw her father look away from Beezus and look directly at her. Did he recognize her? Yes, he did. Mr. Quimby winked. Ramona was shocked. Winking in church! How could her father do such a thing? He winked again and this time held up his thumb and forefinger in a circle. Ramona understood. Her father was telling her he was proud of her, too.

Ramona was filled with joy. Christmas was the most beautiful, magic time of the whole year. Her parents loved her, and she loved them, and Beezus, too. At home there was a Christmas tree and under it, presents, fewer than at past Christmases, but presents all the same. Ramona could not contain her feelings. "B-a-a," she bleated joyfully.

She felt the nudge of a shepherd's crook on the seat of her pajamas and heard her shepherd whisper through clenched teeth, "You be quiet!" Ramona did not bleat again. She wiggled her seat to make her tail wag.

TROUBLE WITH PIES

Tomorrow's Christmas Day: three kinds of pies—
apple, mince, and pumpkin—all same size,
though not much bigger round than hungry eyes.

Since my first try at pie, I cannot choose
between mince, apple, pumpkin; or refuse
one, taking two of all three good twos.

Apple and mince? Apple and pumpkin? What?
Leave pumpkin out, or mince? Well, I guess not!
Pumpkin and mince? No apple have I got.

It would be better—best—to take all three;
but somehow that's not what they say to me.
"Which *do* you want?" they say. I say, "Let's see . . ."

DAVID MCCORD

THE CHRISTMAS PUDDING

Into the basin put the plums,
Stirabout, stirabout, stirabout!

Next the good white flour comes,
Stirabout, stirabout, stirabout!

Sugar and peel and eggs and spice,
Stirabout, stirabout, stirabout!

Mix them and fix them and cook them twice,
Stirabout, stirabout, stirabout!

TRADITIONAL

DUCKLE, DUCKLE, DAISY

Duckle, duckle, daisy
Martha must be crazy,
She went and made a Christmas cake
Of olive oil and gluten-flake,
And put it in the sink to bake,
Duckle, duckle, daisy.

LEROY F. JACKSON

THE ELVES AND THE SHOEMAKER

THE BROTHERS GRIMM
BASED ON A TRANSLATION BY LUCY CRANE

There was once a shoemaker who, through no fault of his own, became so poor that at last he had nothing left but just enough leather to make one pair of shoes. He cut out the shoes that night, so they would be ready to work on the next morning. Then he laid himself quietly down in his bed and fell asleep.

In the morning, after he had said his prayers and was going to get to work, he found the pair of shoes made and finished and standing on his table. He was very astonished and did not know what to think. He took the shoes in his hand to examine them more closely, and they were so well made that every stitch was in its right place, just as if they had come from the hand of a master workman.

Soon a purchaser entered, and as the shoes fitted him very well, he gave more than the usual price for them. Now the shoemaker had enough money to buy leather for two more pairs of shoes. He cut them out at night and intended to set to work the next morning with fresh spirit. But that was not to be, for when he got up they were already finished.

That very day a customer came in and gave him so much money that he was able to buy leather enough for four new pairs. Early the next morning he found the four pairs also finished, and so it always happened; whatever he cut out in the evening was finished by morning, so that soon he was making a good living and became very well-to-do.

One night, not long before Christmas, when the shoemaker had finished cutting the leather for the shoes, and before he went to bed, he said to his wife, "How would it be if we were to sit up tonight and see who it is that does us this service?"

His wife agreed and set a candle to burn. Then they both hid in a corner of the room, behind some coats that were hanging up, and they began to watch. As soon as it was midnight they saw two neatly formed naked little elves come in. They seated themselves before the shoemaker's table, took up the work that was already prepared, and began to stitch, to pierce, and to hammer so cleverly and quickly with their little fingers that the shoemaker's eyes could scarcely follow them, so full of wonder was he. And they never stopped until everything was finished and was standing ready on the table. Then they jumped up and ran off.

The next morning the shoemaker's wife said to her husband, "Those little men have made us rich, and we ought to show that we are grateful. With all their running about, and having nothing to cover them, they must be very cold. I'll tell you what: I will make little shirts, coats, waistcoats, and breeches for them, and knit each of them a pair of stockings, and you shall make each of them a pair of shoes."

The husband consented willingly, and that night, when everything was finished, they laid the gifts together on the table, instead of the cut-out leather. Then they placed themselves so that they could observe how the little men would behave.

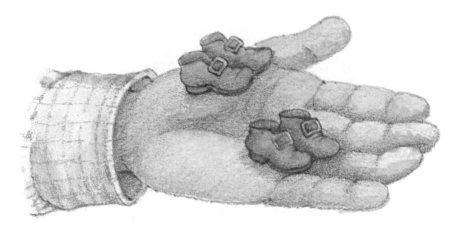

When the clock struck midnight, the elves rushed in, ready to set to work. But when they found, instead of the pieces of prepared leather, the neat little clothes all ready for them, they stood a moment in surprise, and then they showed the greatest delight. Swiftly they took up the pretty garments and slipped them on, singing,

> "What spruce and dandy boys are we!
> No longer cobblers we will be."

Then they hopped and danced about, jumping over the chairs and tables, and at last they danced out the door.

From that time the elves were never seen again. But it always went well with the shoemaker, and he and his wife prospered as long as they lived.

The Puppy Who Wanted a Boy

JANE THAYER

One day Petey, who was a puppy, said to his mother, "I'd like a boy for Christmas."

His mother, who was a dog, said she guessed he could have a boy if he was a very good puppy.

So the day before Christmas, Petey's mother asked, "Have you been a very good puppy?"

"Oh, yes!" said Petey. "I didn't frighten the cat."

"You *didn't*?" asked Petey's mother.

"Well—a—I just frightened her a *little*," said Petey. "And I didn't chew any shoes."

"Not *any*?" said his mother.

"Just a teeny-weeny chew," said Petey.

"All right," said his mother. "I guess you've been good. Anyway, you're awfully little. I shall go out and get you a boy for Christmas."

But when Petey's mother came back, she looked worried.

"How would you like a soft white rabbit with pink ears for Christmas?" she said to Petey.

"No, thanks," said Petey.

"How about some fish? They're nice," said Petey's mother.

"I don't like fish," said Petey. "I'd like a boy."

"Petey," said his mother, "there are no boys to be had. Not one could I find. They're terribly short of boys this year."

Petey felt as if he couldn't stand it if he didn't have a boy.

Finally his mother said, "There, now, there must be a boy somewhere. Perhaps you could find some dog who would give his boy away."

So Petey hopefully started off.

It wasn't long before he saw a collie racing with a boy on a bicycle. Petey trembled with joy.

"If I had a boy on a bicycle," said Petey, "I could run like every-thing! I'll ask the collie politely if he'll give his boy away."

So Petey leaped after the bicycle. He called out to the collie, "Ex-cuse me. Do you want to give your boy away?"

But the collie said *no,* he definitely *didn't,* in a dreadful tone of voice. Petey sat down. He watched the collie and his boy until they were out of his sight.

"I didn't really want a boy on a bicycle anyway," said Petey.

After a while, he saw a red setter playing ball with a boy. Petey was just delighted. "If I had a boy to play ball with," said Petey, "I'd catch the ball smack in my mouth."

But he remembered how cross the collie had been. So he sat down on the sidewalk and called out politely, "Excuse me. Do you want to give your boy away?"

But the setter said *no,* he definitely *didn't,* in a terrifying tone of voice!

"Oh, well," said Petey, trotting off, "I don't think playing ball is much."

After a while he met a Scotty walking with his boy and carrying a package in his mouth.

"Now, that is a good kind of boy!" said Petey. "If I had a boy to carry packages for, there might be some dog biscuits or cookies in the package."

But he remembered how cross the collie and the setter had been. So he stayed across the street and shouted at the top of his lungs, but polite as could be, "Excuse me. Do you want to give your boy away?"

The Scotty had his mouth full of package, but he managed to say *no,* he definitely *didn't,* and he showed his sharp teeth at Petey.

"I guess that wasn't the kind of boy I wanted either," said poor Petey. "But my goodness, where *will* I find a boy?"

Well, Petey went on and on. Up busy streets, dodging the cars, looking in stores and around corners. Down quiet lanes where dogs rushed to their fences and yelped at him. He asked every dog politely. But he couldn't find a single dog who would give his boy away.

Petey's ears began to droop. His tail grew limp. His legs were *so* tired. "My mother was right," he thought. "There isn't a boy to be had."

As it was getting dark, he came to a large building on the very edge of town. Petey was going by very slowly because his paws hurt, when he saw a sign over the door. The sign said: ORPHANS' HOME.

"I know what orphans are," Petey said to himself. "They're children who have no dog to take care of them. Maybe I could find a boy here!"

He padded slowly up the walk. He was so tired he could hardly lift his little paws.

Then Petey stopped. He listened. He could hear music. He looked. Through the window he could see a lighted Christmas tree and children singing carols.

Petey looked some more. On the front step of the orphans' home, all by himself, sat a boy! He looked lonely.

Petey gave a glad little cry. He forgot about being tired. He leaped up the walk and landed in the boy's lap.

Sniff, sniff went Petey's little nose. Wiggle, wag went Petey's tail. He licked the boy with his warm, wet tongue.

How glad the boy was to see Petey! He put both his arms around the little dog and hugged him tight.

Then the front door opened. "Goodness, Dickie," a lady said, "what are you doing out here? Come on in to the Christmas tree."

Petey sat very still. The boy looked up at the lady. Then he looked down at Petey.

The boy said, "I've got a puppy. Can he come too?"

"A puppy!" The lady came over and looked down at Petey. "Why," she said, "you're a nice dog. Wherever did you come from? Yes, bring him in."

"Come on, puppy," said the boy, and in they scampered.

A crowd of boys was playing around the Christmas tree. All the boys rushed at Petey. They all wanted to pick him up. They all wanted to pet him.

Petey wagged his tail. He wagged his fat little body. He frisked about and kissed every boy who came near.

"Can he stay?" the boys asked.

"Yes," said the lady. "He may stay."

"Come on, puppy," Dickie said. "Get your supper."

"We'll fix you a nice warm bed!" cried another boy.

"We'll all play games with you," said a third.

"Who ever would think," said Petey to himself, "that I'd get *fifty* boys for Christmas!"

little tree
little silent Christmas tree
you are so little
you are more like a flower

who found you in the green forest
and were you very sorry to come away?
see   i will comfort you
because you smell so sweetly

i will kiss your cool bark
and hug you safe and tight
just as your mother would,
only don't be afraid

look   the spangles
that sleep all the year in a dark box
dreaming of being taken out and allowed to shine,
the balls the chains red and gold the fluffy threads,

put up your little arms
and i'll give them all to you to hold
every finger shall have its ring
and there won't be a single place dark or unhappy

that when you're quite dressed
you'll stand in the window for everyone to see
and how they'll stare!
oh but you'll be very proud

and my little sister and i will take hands
and looking up at our beautiful tree
we'll dance and sing
"Noel Noel"

E. E. CUMMINGS

The Birth of Jesus

LUKE 2:1–20

And it came to pass in those days, that there went out a decree from Caesar Augustus, that all the world should be taxed. (And this taxing was first made when Cyrenius was governor of Syria.) And all went to be taxed, every one into his own city.

And Joseph also went up from Galilee, out of the city of Nazareth, into Judaea, unto the city of David, which is called Bethlehem; (because he was of the house and lineage of David:) to be taxed with Mary his espoused wife, being great with child.

And so it was, that, while they were there, the days were accomplished that she should be delivered.

And she brought forth her firstborn son, and wrapped him in swaddling clothes, and laid him in a manger; because there was no room for them in the inn.

And there were in the same country shepherds abiding in the field, keeping watch over their flock by night.

And, lo, the angel of the Lord came upon them, and the glory of the Lord shone round about them: and they were sore afraid.

And the angel said unto them, Fear not: for, behold, I bring you good tidings of great joy, which shall be to all people.

For unto you is born this day in the city of David a Savior, which is Christ the Lord.

And this shall be a sign unto you; Ye shall find the babe wrapped in swaddling clothes, lying in a manger.

And suddenly there was with the angel a multitude of the heavenly host praising God, and saying,

Glory to God in the highest, and on earth peace, good will toward men.

And it came to pass, as the angels were gone away from them into heaven, the shepherds said one to another, Let us now go even unto Bethlehem, and see this thing which is come to pass, which the Lord hath made known unto us.

And they came with haste, and found Mary, and Joseph, and the babe lying in a manger.

And when they had seen it, they made known abroad the saying which was told them concerning this child.

And all they that heard it wondered at those things which were told them by the shepherds.

But Mary kept all these things, and pondered them in her heart.

And the shepherds returned, glorifying and praising God for all the things that they had heard and seen, as it was told unto them.

AWAY IN A MANGER

Away in a manger, no crib for a bed,
The little Lord Jesus laid down His sweet head.
The stars in the bright sky looked down where He lay—
The little Lord Jesus asleep on the hay.

The cattle are lowing, the Baby awakes,
But little Lord Jesus, no crying He makes.
I love thee, Lord Jesus! look down from the sky,
And stay by my cradle till morning is nigh.

ATTRIBUTED TO MARTIN LUTHER

WHAT YOU GONNA NAME THAT PRETTY LITTLE BABY?

Oh, Mary, what you gonna name
That pretty little baby?
Glory, glory, glory
To the newborn King!
Some will call Him one thing,
But I think I'll call Him Jesus.
Glory, glory, glory
To the newborn King!
Some will call Him one thing,
But I think I'll say Emmanuel.
Glory, glory, glory
To the newborn King!

SPIRITUAL

BABOUSHKA

RUSSIAN FOLK TALE

It was the night that Jesus was born in Bethlehem. In a faraway country an old woman named Baboushka sat in her snug little house by her warm fire. The wind was drifting the snow outside and howling down the chimney, but it only made Baboushka's fire burn more brightly.

"How glad I am to be indoors," said Baboushka, holding out her hands to the bright blaze.

Suddenly she heard a loud rap at her door. She opened it and there stood three splendidly dressed old men. Their beards were as white as the snow, and so long they almost reached the ground. Their eyes shone kindly in the light of Baboushka's candle, and their arms were full of precious things—boxes of jewels and sweet-smelling oils and ointments.

"We have traveled far, Baboushka," they said, "and we have stopped to tell you of the babe born this night in Bethlehem. He has come to rule the world and teach us to be loving and true. We are bringing Him gifts. Come with us, Baboushka."

Baboushka looked at the swirling, drifting snow and then inside at her cozy room and the crackling fire. "It is too late for me to go with you, good sirs," she said. "The night is too cold." She shut the door and went inside, and the old men journeyed to Bethlehem without her.

But as Baboushka sat rocking by her fire, she began to think about the baby Prince, for she loved babies.

"Tomorrow I will go to find Him," she said, "tomorrow, when it is light, and I will carry Him some toys."

In the morning Baboushka put on her long cloak and took her staff, and she filled her basket with the pretty things a baby would like— gold balls and wooden toys and strings of silver cobwebs—and she set out to find the baby.

But Baboushka had forgotten to ask the three old men the way to Bethlehem, and they had traveled so far during the night that she could not catch up with them. Up and down the road she hurried, through woods and fields and towns, telling everyone she met, "I am looking for the baby Prince. Where does He lie? I have some pretty toys for Him."

But no one could tell her the way. "Farther on, Baboushka, farther on," was their only reply. So she traveled on and on and on for years and years—but she never found the little Prince.

They say that Baboushka is traveling still, looking for Him. And every year, when Christmas Eve comes and all the children are lying fast asleep, Baboushka trudges softly through the snowy fields and towns, wrapped in her long cloak and carrying her basket on her arm. Gently she raps at every door.

"Is He here?" she asks. "Is the baby Prince here?" But the answer is always no, and sorrowfully she starts on her way again. Before she leaves, though, she lays a toy from her basket beside the pillow of each child. "For His sake," she says softly, and then hurries on through the years, forever in search of the baby Prince.

JINGLE BELLS

Dashing through the snow
In a one-horse open sleigh,
O'er the fields we go
Laughing all the way;
Bells on bobtail ring,
Making spirits bright;
Oh, what fun it is to sing
A sleighing song tonight!

Jingle bells! Jingle bells!
Jingle all the way!
Oh, what fun it is to ride in a one-horse open sleigh!
Jingle bells! Jingle bells!
Jingle all the way!
Oh, what fun it is to ride in a one-horse open sleigh!

A day or two ago
I thought I'd take a ride,
And soon Miss Fannie Bright
Was seated by my side;
The horse was lean and lank,
Misfortune seemed his lot,
He got into a drifted bank,
And then we got upsot!

Jingle bells! Jingle bells!
Jingle all the way!
Oh, what fun it is to ride in a one-horse open sleigh!
Jingle bells! Jingle bells!
Jingle all the way!
Oh, what fun it is to ride in a one-horse open sleigh!

JAMES PIERPONT

A Present for Santa Claus

CAROLYN HAYWOOD

There were many signs that Christmas would soon be here. At night the main street looked like fairyland. Tiny electric lights were strung all over the branches of the bare trees. The children talked of Santa Claus and when they would go to see him.

One Saturday morning when Star came into the kitchen for her breakfast, she said to her mother, "Today's the day, isn't it? I'm going to see Santa Claus!"

"That's right," her mother replied.

"When will we go?" Star asked as she sat down to eat her bowl of oatmeal.

"We'll go as soon as I finish clearing up the kitchen," her mother replied.

As soon as Star finished her breakfast, she said, "I'll put my things on and feed the turtles." Star had two turtles that she had named Mabel and Marble.

Star went into her room. She kept her turtles in a glass tank. She picked up a box of turtle food and sprinkled it around the turtles. Then she scratched their backs and said, "Now eat your breakfast. I'm going to see Santa Claus."

When Star and her mother were ready to leave, Star was wearing her blue snow pants and her warm red jacket and cap. Just as her mother opened the door Star cried out, "Oh, Mommy! I haven't any present for Santa Claus."

"You don't take a present to Santa Claus, Star," her mother said. "Santa Claus brings presents to you."

"Oh, but I want a present for him," said Star.

"Now, Star!" said her mother. "Nobody takes presents to Santa Claus."

"But it's Christmas," said Star. "Everybody takes everybody a present."

"Everybody does not take everybody a present," said her mother. "Now come along."

Star shook her head. "Everybody should take Santa Claus a present, because he gives presents to everybody's children. I have to take him a present. Maybe he's like me. Maybe it's his birthday."

Star's mother sat down on the chair beside the door. She held her head and said, "Darling! It is *not* Santa Claus's birthday. You don't have a present for him, you don't need a present for him, and he doesn't want a present."

"Everybody wants presents, Mommy," said Star, almost in tears. "I'll go find something." She darted up the stairs.

She wasn't gone long. When she came down she had a satisfied look on her face. "I'm going to give Mabel to Santa Claus," she said.

"Mabel!" her mother exclaimed. "What will Santa Claus do with Mabel?"

"He'll love Mabel," Star replied.

Star's mother shook her head. "Come along," she said, opening the door. She took Star's hand and hurried her to the bus stop.

When they were seated in the bus, her mother said, "Where is Mabel?"

"In my pocket," Star replied. "In the pocket of my snow pants."

"I hope Mabel's happy in your pocket," her mother said. "It doesn't seem to be the best place for a little turtle."

"She's all right," said Star. "I put my hand in and tickle her every once in a while. Mabel likes being tickled."

"You're sure you want to give her away?" her mother asked. "You've been very fond of your turtles."

"Well, I didn't have time to find anything else for a present for Santa Claus," said Star, "so I went over to Mabel and I said, 'Mabel, you're going to be a present for Santa Claus.' Then I said, 'I guess you don't know about Santa Claus, but he's not a turtle.' "

Star looked up at her mother. "I wanted Mabel to know that he isn't a turtle, so she won't be surprised when she sees him. I told her he's a sort of magic person. And you know something, Mommy?"

"What?" her mother asked.

"Well, once in a fairy story a frog got turned into a handsome prince, so maybe Santa Claus can turn Mabel into a beautiful princess." Star turned and gazed out the window. "She'd be Princess Mabel!" she said with a sigh.

Star's mother sighed, too. Then she said, "I don't believe turning turtles into princesses is exactly Santa Claus's line. He's very busy in the toy business."

Star poked her finger into her pocket and tickled Mabel. "Well, I think I'll call her Princess Mabel anyway."

When Star and her mother reached the store, they went directly to the toy department, where they found Santa Claus. Star stood holding her mother's hand and stared at Santa Claus. There he sat in a big chair on a platform. He looked magnificent in his bright red suit trimmed with white fur and his shiny black boots. He held a little boy on his knee. Star saw the boy whisper into Santa Claus's ear, and she saw Santa Claus's white teeth when he laughed and put the little boy down.

There were several children standing in a line waiting to speak to Santa Claus. Star's mother took her to the end of the line and said, "You wait here until it's your turn to speak to Santa Claus."

"You'll wait with me, won't you, Mommy?" Star asked.

"I'll stand nearby," her mother replied.

"Where shall I put my present for Santa Claus?" Star asked. "He doesn't have any Christmas tree."

"Well, you certainly couldn't hang Mabel on a Christmas tree, even if he had one," said her mother. "You see, Star, none of these children have presents for Santa Claus."

"That's because they forgot," said Star as she moved forward in the line.

Star watched as the children ahead of her reached Santa Claus. Some he took on his lap and some stood by his knee. When the little boy ahead of her began to talk to Santa Claus, Star put her hand into her pocket. She was surprised, for she couldn't find Mabel. She thought perhaps she had forgotten which pocket she had put her in, so she dug into her other one. Mabel was not there.

Now the little boy had gone, and Santa Claus was beckoning to Star. She was still poking around in her pocket when she reached his knee.

"Hello!" said Santa Claus in his big, cheery voice. "What's your name?"

"I'm Star," she replied, just as her finger went through a hole in her pocket.

Santa Claus leaned over and said, "What seems to be the matter?"

"I brought you a present," Star replied, "but I can't find it." Star dug down and made the hole in her pocket bigger.

"What is it you're trying to find?" Santa Claus asked.

"Mabel!" Star replied.

"Oh!" said Santa Claus.

"I guess she fell through the hole in my pocket," said Star, leaning over like a jackknife. Then she unzipped the bottom of the leg of her snow pants. She straightened up and said, "I'll shake my leg, and maybe she'll fall out."

"That's the thing!" said Santa Claus. "Shake a leg!"

Star shook and then she jumped while everyone stood around and watched her. Mabel did not appear. "I'll find her," said Star. "She's hiding!"

Star sat down on the floor beside Santa Claus's big black boots. She felt inside the leg of her pants and suddenly her face broke into a wide smile. "I found her!" she said, looking up at Santa Claus.

"Good!" said Santa Claus. "I can't wait to see Mabel."

Star leaned against Santa Claus's knee. "Hold out your hand," she said. Santa Claus held out his big hand, and Star placed the tiny turtle on her back in his palm. "I hope she's all right," said Star. "If she kicks her legs, she's alive."

Santa Claus's great big head in his red cap bent over his hand as Star leaned against him. Their heads were together as they watched to see if Mabel would kick her legs. Suddenly Star cried out, "She's alive! Mabel's alive!"

"Sure enough!" said Santa Claus. "She's alive and kicking!"

Star looked up into Santa Claus's face. "I'm sorry I couldn't wrap up your present," she said. "You don't mind if Mabel isn't wrapped up, do you?"

Santa Claus drew Star to him and gave her a great big hug. "I never had a nicer present than Mabel," he said. "Thank you, and a merry Christmas to you."

As she walked away Star turned and looked back at Santa Claus. He waved his hand. Star waved too and called back, "Mabel likes hamburger! Just a teenie-weenie bit, of course."

"I'll remember," Santa Claus promised. "Hamburger for her Christmas dinner!"

On Christmas morning, when Star went to the fireplace in the living room, standing on the hearth was a beautiful doll dressed like a princess with a crown on her head. A card stood beside her. It said:

THIS IS PRINCESS MABEL, FROM SANTA CLAUS

THE MORE IT SNOWS

The more it
SNOWS-tiddely-pom,
The more it
GOES-tiddely-pom
The more it
GOES-tiddely-pom
On
Snowing.

And nobody
KNOWS-tiddely-pom,
How cold my
TOES-tiddely-pom
How cold my
TOES-tiddely-pom
Are
Growing.

A. A. MILNE

42

SNOWFLAKES

I once thought that snowflakes were feathers
    And that they came falling down
When the Moon Lady feathered her chickens
    And shook out her silver gown.

And then I began to look closer,
    And now I know just what they are—
I caught one today in my mitten,
    And there was a baby star.

MARCHETTE CHUTE

MERRY CHRISTMAS

I saw on the snow
when I tried my skis
the track of a mouse
beside some trees.

Before he tunneled
to reach his house
he wrote "Merry Christmas"
in white, in mouse.

AILEEN FISHER

THE CHRISTMAS THIEF

JAY WILLIAMS

It was the day before Christmas in the little town of Sterkdam in Holland, but everyone was sad. Holland and Spain were at war. Spanish soldiers, armed with muskets and swords, surrounded the town. Worse still, twelve great cannons shot iron balls over the town walls, battering houses and knocking down chimneys. But the brave people of Sterkdam refused to surrender.

They kept their town gates closed so that the Spaniards could not enter, but at the same time, the Spaniards would let no one leave. Food began to run short, and soon there was nothing left to eat. Everyone was hungry, from the mayor in his fine house to the only prisoner in the town jail.

This prisoner's name was Tyl Uilenspiegel, and he was a famous thief. It was said that he could steal the eggs from under a sitting hen, or the spectacles off your nose. In Sterkdam there was little to steal, and Tyl had let the officers arrest him and put him in prison so that he would have food and shelter for the winter. Now, however, they could not give him so much as a crust of bread.

He stood at the barred window, looked at the clear blue sky, and sighed. A boy walked by in the street below, hugging his stomach and weeping. Tyl heard him and looked down. "What's the matter with you?" he asked.

"I'm hungry," said the boy, "and tomorrow is Christmas. There will be no presents and no Christmas dinner. Not even Saint Nicholas could get into this town with the Spaniards all around it."

Tyl stared at the boy and thought about all the hungry children of Sterkdam. "Maybe I can do something about it," he said. "Get me a pail of blue paint and a brush, and come back here as quickly as you can."

Away sped the boy. Soon he returned with the paint and brush. Around his waist Tyl always carried a long, thin cord. He uncoiled it now and lowered it through the bars.

"Put the brush in the pail and tie the handle of the pail to the cord," he said.

When the boy had done so, Tyl pulled up the pail. He painted the bars of his window blue; then he stood in a corner behind the cell door and shouted, loudly, "Good-bye! I'm going!"

The guard heard him and came running. He unlocked the door and opened it. When he looked in he saw a window without bars—for the blue bars did not show against the blue sky. "The prisoner has escaped!" he cried, and rushed off for help, leaving the cell door open. Tyl strolled quietly out of the prison and into the street, taking with him a sheet from his bed.

There were people guarding the walls of the town, and there were more people guarding the great main gate. And there was one man with a musket guarding the little iron door that opened onto the river.

Tyl walked up to him and said, "What are you doing?"

The guard straightened. "My orders are not to let anyone in through the gate," he replied.

"Very good," said Tyl. "Then open it, for I am already in, and I am going out."

The man unbolted the gate. "The Spaniards will kill you," he warned.

"They will if they see me," said Tyl, "but I won't let them see me."

He put the bed sheet over his head. Against the white snow he was invisible. He walked to the frozen river and crossed it.

In the Spanish camp the soldiers were preparing their Christmas Eve feast, roasting meat and cooking good stews in big iron pots over blazing bonfires. Tyl crept up to the back of the nearest tent, and with a tiny knife slit the canvas. He peeped in; there was no one inside. He stepped through the slit. When he came out of the front of the tent, he was wearing a Spanish helmet and breastplate and carrying a big cloak over one arm.

He walked boldly to one of the fires and helped himself to a piece of roast meat. One of the soldiers stopped him and said, "Where are you going with that?"

"It is for the general," answered Tyl in his best Spanish. He put the meat into the cloak. He went to another fire and took a roast chicken. "For the general," he said.

When he could carry no more, he found a quiet corner and hid the food. Then off he went again with the empty cloak—as lightly as a feather, as quietly as a puff of smoke—taking candies and cakes,

strings of sausages, loaves of bread, round hard cheeses, roast geese, legs of lamb, and slices of beef.

From the general's tent, Tyl took an enormous Christmas pudding. As he was leaving with the pudding wrapped in his cloak, a soldier said, "Wait. What have you there?"

"A present from the general to the captain," said Tyl, and went on his way.

As darkness fell, the Spaniards deserted their posts to eat dinner. Tyl went up to the first cannon. It was loaded and ready, pointing at the town wall. He took out the cannonball and in its place crammed a bundle of food. He did the same to the next cannon, and the next, until all twelve were filled with food instead of cannonballs. Then he went looking for the captain of artillery.

"Sir," said Tyl, saluting. "I bring a message from the general. You are to fire all your cannons at the city tonight to show the people of Sterkdam they can have no rest."

"But how can we aim in the darkness?" asked the captain of artillery.

"I will sneak into the town and light a torch in the church tower," said Tyl. "You can aim at the light, and you must fire all the cannons together, just once."

"You are a brave man," said the captain.

"I know," said Tyl modestly. "Be ready for my signal." He took off the helmet and armor. Then, like the shadow of an owl, he slipped back across the river.

Near the town walls stood a tall windmill, its sails turning slowly in the night breeze. Tyl jumped up and caught the lowest sail. Up he went, higher and higher, until he was level with the top of the wall. Then he leaped with all his might and fell sprawling on the hard stone. No one saw him. The town was quiet. The hungry people had gone to bed early.

Tyl climbed down and made his way to the town square. There he pounded on people's doors, shouting, "Wake up! Wake up! Come out! Come out!"

Windows flew open. People looked and shouted, "What is it? What's happening?" They came into the street with swords and torches and lanterns, thinking the Spanish army was attacking.

Tyl snatched a torch from someone and ran up the steps of the church. He stood before the door where everyone could see him. "Listen!" he cried. "Saint Nicholas is coming."

The mayor was there in his nightcap. "It's the thief, Tyl Uilenspiegel," he exclaimed. "Seize him! Arrest him!"

"Wait—" Tyl began.

But several men were already advancing on him, swords ready. Tyl turned, ran into the church, slammed the door in their faces, and bolted it.

Up the tower stairs he raced, until he came to the top where the great bells hung. He leaned out, waving his torch. The townspeople stared up at him with their mouths open.

"Shoot him," commanded the mayor. "He is signaling to the enemy."

Muskets were raised; men took aim. But before they could fire a shot—*boom!* came the crash of the Spanish cannons. And out of the sky fell roast geese, roast chickens, roast beef, and loaves of bread. Nuts and candies pattered down like hail; cheeses bounced off the rooftops. A leg of lamb fell into a woman's arms. A string of sausages wrapped itself around a man's neck. The general's plum pudding hit the mayor on the head, knocking him flat.

"Merry Christmas!" yelled Tyl, leaning from the tower.

Everyone cheered and hurried to pick up the good things. Then a bonfire was lit in the square, and the people of Sterkdam feasted until dawn.

As the bells rang out on Christmas morning, an army of Hollanders came marching across the plains toward the town. There were too many of them for the Spaniards, who ran away without a fight—leaving their tents, their cooking pots, and even their cannons behind. The gates of the town were opened at last, and the people welcomed their friends with joy.

That night, in a solemn ceremony, the mayor hung a golden chain around Tyl's neck. On it was a golden medal inscribed with these words:

TO THE THIEF TYL UILENSPIEGEL WHO STOLE CHRISTMAS FOR THE PEOPLE OF STERKDAM

ONCE THERE WAS A SNOWMAN

Once there was a snowman
   Who stood outside the door.
He wished that he could come inside
   And run about the floor.
He wished that he could warm himself
   Beside the fire, so red.
He wished that he could climb
   Upon the big white bed.

So he called to the North Wind,
   "Come and help me, pray,
For I'm completely frozen
   Standing out here all day."
So the North Wind came along
   And blew him in the door,
And now there's nothing left of him
   But a puddle on the floor!

ANONYMOUS

50

A SLED FOR CHRISTMAS

UP! UP! Up I jump
and down the stairs I fly.
LOOK! LOOK! A brand-new sled
that I can't wait to try.

ZIP! ZIP! Bundle up,
I'm toasty warm inside.
QUICK! QUICK! Out the door,
then down the hill I'll glide.

NO! NO! It isn't fair,
it simply isn't right.
SNOW! SNOW! I see no snow,
it melted overnight.

JACK PRELUTSKY

The Little Blue Dishes

ANONYMOUS

Once upon a time there was a poor woodcutter who lived with his wife and three children in a forest in Germany. There was a big boy called Hans and a little boy named Peterkin and a little sister named Gretchen, just five years old. When Christmas was getting near, the children went to the toy shop to look at all of the toys.

"Gretchen," said Peterkin, "what do you like best?"

"Oh! That little box of blue dishes," said Gretchen. "That is the very best of all."

On Christmas Eve the children hung up their stockings, although their mother had said that they were so poor they could not have much this Christmas. Hans ran out after supper to play with the big boys. Gretchen and Peterkin sat talking before the fire about the Christmas toys and especially about the box of blue dishes. By and by Gretchen ran off to bed and was soon asleep. Peterkin ran to look in his bank. There was only one penny, but he took it and ran quickly to the toy shop.

"What have you for a penny?" he said to the toy man.

"Only a small candy heart with a picture on it," said the man.

"But I want that set of blue dishes," said Peterkin.

"Oh, they cost ten cents," said the man.

So Peterkin bought the candy heart and put it in Gretchen's stocking, and then he ran off to bed.

Pretty soon Hans came home. He was cold and hungry. When he saw Gretchen's stocking he peeked in, then put his hand in and drew out the candy heart. "Oh," said Hans, "how good this smells," and before you could say a word he had eaten the candy heart. "Oh, dear," he said, "that was for Gretchen for Christmas. I'll run and buy something else for her." So he ran to his bank and he had ten pennies. Quickly he ran to the toy store.

"What have you got for ten pennies?" he asked the storekeeper.

"Well, I'm almost sold out," said the toy man, "but here in this little box is a set of blue dishes."

"I will take them," said Hans, and home he ran and dropped the dishes into Gretchen's stocking. Then he went to bed.

Early in the morning the children came running downstairs.

"Oh!" said Gretchen. "Look at my stocking!" And when she saw the blue dishes, she was as happy as could be. But Peterkin could never understand how his candy heart had changed into a box of blue dishes.

Long, Long Ago

Winds through the olive trees
    Softly did blow,
Round little Bethlehem
    Long, long ago.

Sheep on the hillside lay
    Whiter than snow;
Shepherds were watching them,
    Long, long ago.

Then from the happy sky,
    Angels bent low,
Singing their songs of joy,
    Long, long ago.

For in a manger bed,
    Cradled we know,
Christ came to Bethlehem,
    Long, long ago.

ANONYMOUS

What Can I Give Him?

What can I give Him,
    Poor as I am?
If I were a shepherd
    I would bring a lamb,
If I were a Wise Man
    I would do my part—
Yet what I can, I give Him,
    Give my heart.

CHRISTINA ROSSETTI

How Far Is It to Bethlehem?

How far is it to Bethlehem?
  Not very far.
Shall we find the stable-room
  Lit by the star?

Can we see the little child,
  Is He within?
If we lift the wooden latch
  May we go in?

May we stroke the creatures there,
  Ox, ass, or sheep?
May we peer like them and see
  Jesus asleep?

If we touch His tiny hand
  Will He awake?
Will He know we've come so far
  Just for His sake?

God, in His mother's arms,
  Babes in the byre,
Sleep, as they sleep who find
  Their heart's desire.

FRANCES A. CHESTERTON

The Friendly Beasts

Jesus, our brother, strong and good,
Was humbly born in a stable rude;
And the friendly beasts around Him stood,
Jesus, our brother, strong and good.

"I," said the sheep with curly horn,
"I gave Him my wool for His blanket warm.
"He wore my coat on Christmas morn,
"I," said the sheep with curly horn.

"I," said the dove from rafters high.
"I cooed Him to sleep so He would not cry,
"We cooed Him to sleep, my mate and I;
"I," said the dove from rafters high.

"I," said the cow, all white and red.
"I gave Him my manger for His bed;
"I gave Him my hay to pillow His head;
"I," said the cow, all white and red.

"I," said the donkey, shaggy and brown.
"I carried His mother uphill and down;
"I carried her safely to Bethlehem town,
"I," said the donkey, shaggy and brown.

And every beast, by some good spell,
In the stable dark was glad to tell,
Of the gift he gave Emmanuel,
The gift he gave Emmanuel.

ENGLISH CAROL

JESUS AHATONHIA (JESUS IS BORN)

'Twas in the moon of wintertime when all
   the birds had fled,
That mighty Gitchi Manitou sent angel choirs instead.
Before their light the stars grew dim, and
   wand'ring hunters heard the hymn
"Jesus, your King, is born; Jesus is born: in excelsis gloria!"

Within a lodge of broken bark the tender Babe
   was found,
A ragged robe of rabbit skin enwrapped His
   beauty round.
And as the hunter braves drew nigh, the
   angels' song rang loud and high;
"Jesus, your King, is born; Jesus is born: in excelsis gloria!"

The earliest moon of wintertime is not so round and fair
As was the ring of glory on the helpless Infant
   there.
And Chiefs from far before Him knelt with gifts
   of fox and beaver pelt.
"Jesus, your King, is born; Jesus is born: in excelsis gloria!"

Oh children of the forest free, oh sons of Manitou,
The Holy Child of earth and heaven is born
   today for you.
Come kneel before the radiant Boy, who brings you
   beauty, peace, and joy.
"Jesus, your King, is born; Jesus is born: in excelsis gloria!"

FATHER JEAN DE BRÉFEUF, TRANSLATED FROM THE HURON LANGUAGE

UNCLE WIGGILY'S CHRISTMAS

HOWARD R. GARIS

"Only three more days until Christmas!" called Susie Littletail. "Aren't you glad, Uncle Wiggily?"

"Indeed I am," Uncle Wiggily answered. "Very glad!"

Johnnie and Billie Bushytail, the squirrels, looked from the window of their house. Johnnie held up a string of nuts that he was getting ready to put on the Christmas tree.

"Billie and I are going to help Santa Claus!" chattered Johnnie.

"Good!" Uncle Wiggily laughed. "Santa Claus needs help!"

The bunny uncle hopped along through the snow until he reached the kennel of Jackie and Peetie Bow Wow, the puppy dog boys.

"We're popping corn!" barked Jackie. "Getting ready for Christmas! That's why we can't be out!"

The bunny had not gone very much farther before he heard some children talking behind a bush around which the snow was piled in a high drift. Uncle Wiggily could hide behind this drift and hear what was said.

"Is Santa Claus coming to your house?" asked one boy of another.

"I don't guess so," was the answer. "My father said our chimney was so full of black soot that Santa Claus couldn't get down. He'd look like a charcoal man if he did, I guess."

"It's the same way at our house," sighed the first boy. "Our chimney is all stopped up. I guess there'll be no Christmas presents this year."

"My! That's too bad!" thought Uncle Wiggily to himself. "There ought to be a Christmas for everyone, and a little thing like a soot-filled chimney ought not to stand in the way. All the animal children whom I know are going to get presents. I wish I could help these boys. And they probably have sisters, also, who will get nothing for Christmas. Too bad!"

Uncle Wiggily peered over the top of the snowbank. He saw the boys, but they did not notice the rabbit, and Uncle Wiggily knew where the boys lived.

"I wish I could help those boys who are not going to have any Christmas," said the bunny gentleman to himself as he hopped on.

And just then, in the air overhead, he heard the sounds of "Caw! Caw! Caw!"

"Crows!" exclaimed Uncle Wiggily. "My friends the black crows! They stay here all winter. Black crows—black—black—why, a chimney is black inside, just as a crow is black outside! I'm beginning to think of something! Yes, that's what I am!"

The rabbit's pink nose began twinkling very fast. It always did when he was thinking, and now it was sparkling almost like a star on a frosty night.

"Ha! I have it!" exclaimed Uncle Wiggily. "A crow can become no blacker inside a sooty chimney than outside! If Santa Claus can't go down a black chimney, why a crow can! I'll have these crows pretend to be St. Nicholas!"

No sooner thought of than done! Uncle Wiggily put his paws to his lips and sent out a shrill whistle, just as a policeman does when he wants the automobiles to stop turning somersaults.

"Caw! Caw! Caw!" croaked the black crows high in the white, snowy air. "Uncle Wiggily is calling us," said the head crow. "Caw! Caw!"

Down they flew, perching on the bare limbs of trees in the wood not far from the bunny's hollow stump bungalow.

"How do you do, Crows!" greeted the rabbit. "I called you because I want you to take a few Christmas presents to some boys who, otherwise, will not get any. Their chimneys are choked with black soot!"

"Black soot will not bother us," said the largest crow of all. "We don't mind going down the blackest chimney in the world!"

"I thought you wouldn't," said Uncle Wiggily. "That's why I called you. Now, of course, I know that the kind of presents that Santa Claus will bring to the animal children will not all be such as real boys and girls would like. But still there are some which may do.

"I can get willow whistles made by Grandpa Lightfoot, the old squirrel gentleman. I can get wooden puzzles gnawed from the aspen tree by Grandpa Whackum, the beaver. Grandpa Goosey Gander and I will gather the round brown balls from the sycamore tree, and the boys can use them for marbles."

"Those will be very nice presents indeed," cawed a middle-sized crow. "The boys ought to like them."

"And will you take the things down the black chimneys?" asked Uncle Wiggily. "I'll give you some of Nurse Jane Fuzzy Wuzzy's thread so you may easily carry the whistles, puzzles, wooden marbles, and other presents."

"We'll take them down the chimneys!" cawed the crows. "It matters not to us how much black soot there is! It will not show on our black wings."

So among his friends Uncle Wiggily gathered up bundles of woodland presents. And in the dusk of Christmas Eve the black crows fluttered silently in from the forest, gathered up in their claws the presents which the bunny had tied with thread, and away they flapped, not only to the houses of the two boys but also to the homes of some girls about whom Uncle Wiggily had heard. Their chimneys, too, it seemed, were choked with soot.

But the crows could be made no blacker, not even if you dusted them with charcoal, so they did not in the least mind fluttering down the sooty chimneys. And so softly did they make their way that not a boy or girl heard them! As silently and as quietly as Santa Claus himself went the crows!

All during Christmas Eve they fluttered down the chimneys at the homes of poor boys and girls, helping St. Nicholas, until all the presents that Uncle Wiggily had gathered from his friends had been put in place.

Then, throughout Woodland, great changes took place. Firefly lights began to glow on Christmas trees. Mysterious bundles seemed to come from nowhere, and took their places under the trees, in stockings, and on chairs or mantels.

And then night came, and all was still, and quiet, and dark—as dark as the black crows or the soot in the chimneys.

But in the morning, when the stars had faded and the moon was pale, the glorious sun came up and made the snow sparkle like ten million billion diamonds.

"Merry Christmas, Uncle Wiggily!" called Nurse Jane. "See what Santa Claus brought me."

"Merry Christmas, Nurse Jane!" answered the bunny. "And what a fine lot of presents St. Nicholas left for me! See them!"

"Oh, isn't he a great old chap!" laughed Nurse Jane as she smelled a bottle of perfume.

And all over the land voices could be heard saying, "Merry Christmas! Merry Christmas!"

Near the hearth in the homes of some boys and girls who had not gone to bed with happy thoughts of the morrow were some delightful presents. How they opened their eyes and stared—these boys and girls who had expected no Christmas.

"Why! Why!" exclaimed one of the two lads whom Uncle Wiggily had heard talking near the snowbank. "How in the world did Santa Claus get down our black chimney?"

But of course they knew nothing of Uncle Wiggily and the crows. And please don't you tell them.

A VISIT FROM ST. NICHOLAS

'Twas the night before Christmas, when all through the house
Not a creature was stirring, not even a mouse.
The stockings were hung by the chimney with care,
In hopes that St. Nicholas soon would be there.
The children were nestled all snug in their beds,
While visions of sugarplums danced in their heads;
And Mamma in her kerchief and I in my cap,
Had just settled our brains for a long winter's nap—
When out on the lawn there arose such a clatter
I sprang from my bed to see what was the matter.
Away to the window I flew like a flash,
Tore open the shutters and threw up the sash.
The moon on the breast of the new-fallen snow
Gave a luster of midday to objects below;
When what to my wondering eyes should appear
But a miniature sleigh and eight tiny reindeer,

With a little old driver, so lively and quick,
I knew in a moment it must be St. Nick!
More rapid than eagles his coursers they came,
And he whistled and shouted and called them by name.
"Now, Dasher! now, Dancer! now, Prancer and Vixen!
On, Comet! on, Cupid! on, Donder and Blitzen!
To the top of the porch, to the top of the wall,
Now, dash away, dash away, dash away, all!"
As dry leaves that before the wild hurricane fly,
When they meet with an obstacle mount to the sky,
So up to the housetop the coursers they flew,
With a sleigh full of toys—and St. Nicholas, too.
And then, in a twinkling, I heard on the roof
The prancing and pawing of each little hoof.

As I drew in my head and was turning around,
Down the chimney St. Nicholas came with a bound.
He was dressed all in fur from his head to his foot,
And his clothes were all tarnished with ashes and soot.
A bundle of toys he had flung on his back,
And he looked like a peddler just opening his pack.
His eyes, how they twinkled! His dimples, how merry!
His cheeks were like roses, his nose like a cherry;
His droll little mouth was drawn up like a bow,
And the beard on his chin was as white as the snow.
The stump of a pipe he held tight in his teeth,
And the smoke, it encircled his head like a wreath.

He had a broad face and a little round belly
That shook, when he laughed, like a bowlful of jelly.
He was chubby and plump—a right jolly old elf:
And I laughed when I saw him, in spite of myself;
A wink of his eye and a twist of his head
Soon gave me to know I had nothing to dread.
He spoke not a word, but went straight to his work,
And filled all the stockings; then turned with a jerk,
And laying his finger aside of his nose,
And giving a nod, up the chimney he rose.
He sprang to his sleigh, to his team gave a whistle,
And away they all flew like the down of a thistle.
But I heard him exclaim, ere he drove out of sight,
"Happy Christmas to all, and to all a good night!"

CLEMENT CLARKE MOORE

The Bells

Hear the sledges with the bells—
    Silver bells!
What a world of merriment their melody foretell!
How they tinkle, tinkle, tinkle,
    In the icy air of night!
While the stars that oversprinkle
All the heavens seem to twinkle
    With a crystalline delight;
Keeping time, time, time,
In a sort of Runic rhyme,
To the tintinnabulation that so musically wells
From the bells, bells, bells, bells,
    Bells, bells, bells—
From the jingling and the tinkling of the bells.

EDGAR ALLAN POE

Carol of the Russian Children

Snowbound mountains,
Snowbound valleys,
Snowbound plateaus, clad in white.
Fur-robed moujiks, fur-robed nobles,
Fur-robed children, see the light.

Shaggy pony, shaggy oxen,
Gentle shepherds wait the light;
Little Jesu, little mother,
Good St. Joseph, come this night.
Light! Light! Light!

ANONYMOUS

WE WISH YOU A MERRY CHRISTMAS

We wish you a merry Christmas
And a happy New Year;
A pocket full of money
And a cellar full of beer,
And a great fat pig
To last you all the year.

ENGLISH CAROL

WASSAIL SONG

God bless the master of this house,
Likewise the mistress too.
May their barns be filled with wheat and corn
And their hearts be always true.

A merry Christmas is our wish
Where'er we do appear,
To you a well-filled purse, a well-filled dish,
And a happy bright New Year!

ENGLISH CAROL

THE CHRISTMAS WHALE

ROGER DUVOISIN

What a blustering, freezing, nipping wind blew at the North Pole that year! Snowdrifts piled so high around Santa's igloo that the red chimney, sticking out, looked like a red cherry on the top of a cream pie. Santa had to dig a tunnel to come out of the house; and each day he had to make the tunnel longer, for the snow would not stop falling.

"I daresay it's worse than the blizzard of eighty-eight," said Santa, coming out of the tunnel one day.

Small wonder that in such weather Blitzen the reindeer suddenly felt a chill run down his back and had to be put to bed with aspirin, hot tea, and a hot-water bottle.

Small wonder that Vixen, in the middle of a game of solitaire . . .

Then Comet as he was practicing on the flute . . .

72

And then all of Santa's reindeer, one after the other, felt the chill down their backs and had to be put to bed with aspirin, hot tea, and hot-water bottles. It was a flu epidemic.

"Curse the snow and the wind and the cold and the flu!" cried Santa. "They *would* do that to my reindeer just before Christmas!" And Santa sat at his desk to telephone to his doctor: "Get your dog sleigh ready and come over at once. It's urgent!"

When the doctor came in, Santa trotted behind him from bed to bed, looking very worried.

"Well, nothing very grave," said the doctor after taking the last reindeer's temperature. "Two or three weeks in bed and everything will be all right."

"All right?" exclaimed Santa, wringing his hands in despair. "All right, with Christmas only a week away! But that's a catastrophe! What shall I do? Who will draw my sleigh? That's a catastrophe!"

"A catastrophe," repeated Santa when the doctor had left. "That's what it is—a catastrophe." And he brooded so much that Mrs. Santa called him four times for lunch before he even heard.

"Now, don't despair, and eat your soup before it's cold," said Mrs. Santa. "You still have eight long days to find a way out of your troubles."

"Eight days," Santa lamented after dinner. "That's a real catastrophe.

"By all the chimneys! By all the stockings! By all the Christmas trees in all the world! That's a *catastrophic* catastrophe!"

While Santa thus lamented and walked back and forth in his igloo with no idea coming to him, all his friends, the North Pole animals, talked of nothing but the flu epidemic and the coming Christmas.

"Poor old Santa," they said to one another. "Imagine his missing the first Christmas in five hundred years! And with all these toys and gifts piled up in the big shed! Couldn't we find a way to help him?"

"Ah," said the huskies, "if we could only fly, wouldn't we draw Santa's sleigh through the skies! But we can't, alas."

"Ah," said the white bears, "if we could swim like the porpoises, we would make a boat out of the sleigh and draw it through the waves. But we can't, alas."

"Ah," said the walruses and the seals, "if we could gallop fast like the wind we would sweep the sleigh round the world. But we can't, alas."

"And us gulls," said the gulls, "if we were as strong as albatrosses, *we* would draw the sleigh. But we aren't, alas."

"Well," said the cod (he was full of good fish sense), "fine intentions won't help Santa. What he needs is one idea with no ifs in it. And, mind you, *I* have one."

The cod called Santa, who was still walking back and forth by himself, now in his igloo, now at the edge of the ice, and said: "Stop walking and muttering for a moment and listen to me, Santa, and your worries will swim away like frightened sardines. What you want is something fast enough, strong enough, to carry your packages round the world. I have that thing for you—the whale! Her back is as broad as an iceberg, she is as strong as the waves in a storm, and she is as fast as the wind. Go and ask her."

"My little cod," said Santa, "I think that you are the cleverest fish in all the seas. I am going to see the whale right now."

The whale was playing far away among the gray waves, and Santa whistled and tramped and shouted almost until dinnertime before she noticed him. Then she came at once, splashing the icy water around her. She got Santa all wet.

She was indeed kind and obliging. "I am ready. When do I start?" she said simply when she heard what Santa wanted.

The very next day Santa rubbed his hands with joy while the walruses, the seals, the white bears, and the gulls came to fetch the mountain of Christmas packages which stood in the big shed. One by one the packages were carried away to the water's edge to be piled into a new mountain on the broad back of the kindly whale.

So many boxes were brought up that the kindly whale stood lower and lower in the water.

"Watch my water line," she warned. "Don't let me sink below it. I've got to breathe, you know." She was so frightened that she would not let Santa put a last little box of building blocks on the top of the mountain. It was all safely tied up with Christmas ribbons.

"We'll take it next year," said Santa.

While the white bears, the walruses, the seals, the gulls, and Mrs. Santa cheered, Santa and the kindly whale departed.

Santa was so happy that he whistled "Jingle Bells" almost all the way to New York, which was the first stop.

Upon their arrival in New York a pilot climbed upon the head of the kindly whale to lead her into the harbor toward two little tugboats, which waited to push her gently to the pier.

The pier soon looked like an ant nest, with little men running to and fro, carrying packages on their backs, while the customs officers watched with indulgent smiles and never opened as much as one package for inspection.

From New York, Santa and the kindly whale went to South America, and to Africa and to Europe, and to Australia.

And then, very weary, but very happy, they went back home to the North Pole, knowing that in spite of the flu, gift giving would go on that Christmas just as it had for the past years.

The icy cold water of the North never felt so deliciously refreshing to the kindly whale, just as the odor of the hot leek soup which Mrs. Santa had prepared for Santa never seemed more appetizing to him.

"Really," he said to Mrs. Santa as she helped him put on his warm slippers, "I have found whale traveling extremely convenient. If there were not so many pictures and stories about my reindeer and me, I would ask the kindly whale more often. After all, on Christmas cards, I would look just as glorious riding a whale as I do driving my sleigh. Whales are very decorative."

THANK-YOU NOTE

I wanted small pierced earrings (gold).
You gave me slippers (gray).
My mother said that she would scold
Unless I wrote to say
How much I liked them.

Not much.

JUDITH VIORST

THE TARDY SANTA CLAUS

I am a little Santa Claus
Who somehow got belated;
My reindeer didn't come in time,
And so of course I waited.
I found your chimneys plastered tight,
Your stockings put away,
I heard you talking of the gifts
You had on Christmas Day;
So will you please to take me in
And keep me till November?
I'd rather start Thanksgiving Day
Than miss you *next* December!

KATE D. WIGGIN

A WOMAN NAMED MRS. S. CLAUS

A woman named Mrs. S. Claus
Deserves to be heard from because
    She sits in her den
    Baking gingerbread men
While her husband gets all the applause.

J. PATRICK LEWIS

THE THREE MAGI

PURA BELPRÉ

It was the fifth of January, the eve of the Three Kings' Day, the day when all Spanish children eagerly await their Christmas presents. In the sumptuous Palace of the Orient, where the Magi Kings lived, there was excitement and confusion. The royal doorman had been busy all morning answering the bell as the couriers came from the four corners of the world, bringing the royal mail. Inside the palace the Lord Chamberlain's voice gave orders to his hundred servants.

"Open the windows!" he shouted, and a hundred men, in uniforms decked with gold and silver in which the initials M.M. (Magi Messengers) stood out, ran from one side of the spacious hall to the other, and opened wide the royal windows, letting in the cool air.

In the royal kitchen of the Three Magi, the innumerable cooks were getting ready an immense repast for a long journey.

Outside the palace in the royal stables, the stamping and neighing of the royal horses could be heard for miles around. Lines and lines of coaches, covered with heavy blankets, could be seen down the hall.

"There comes Carlos the stable boy again," whispered a dapple gray horse to another.

"Stop your stamping, stop it this minute," called out Carlos as he opened the door.

In reply, the horses raised their heads and neighed loudly and resonantly.

"I know, I know," said Carlos, "but this is the eve of the Three Kings' Day, and it's the camels the Magi want and not horses. Stop your neighing. Stop your stamping."

Slowly he opened the door and led the camels to the public square. Already people were gathered there, while the stable hands brought gallons of water, baskets of scented soaps, and a great number of combs and brushes.

The royal camels were about to receive their bath and this was a ceremony always performed in public. First, the water was poured over their backs. Then the stable boys divided into groups of ten and, armed with soap and brushes, began the scrubbing. This finished, another group would begin the combing and smoothing of the hair. Decked then with red mantles and silver reins, the three choice stable boys, Carlos, Juan, and Pedro, led them to the door of the royal palace. The three magnificent-looking camels of the Three Magi were the happiest camels in the entire world, for it was the fifth of January and they were to carry on their backs the three most wished-for persons in the children's world—King Gaspar, King Melchor, and King Baltazar. But they were impatient as they stood there. Putting their three heads together, they asked each other, "Where are the Three Magi? Why are they keeping us waiting?"

And well might they ask, for the Three Kings could hardly be seen.

In the Grand Throne Room, behind a barricade of opened envelopes, they sat, laughing and nodding at each other as they read and carefully put away millions of letters sent them. There were letters of all sizes and colors. Some of them were written on new paper with gilt borders, others embellished with flowers and birds, written in clear and legible handwriting, but the majority of them—and these were the ones the Kings liked best—were written on scraps of paper, and full of blots of ink and many erasures. They all carried the same message—a plea for a special toy and a promise to be a better boy or girl in the future.

Finally, the last letter was read and carefully put away. Slowly the Three Magi rose from their beautiful thrones and left the room. Majestic in their bearing, handsomely garbed with precious stones and jewelry, and with their ermine coats about them, the Three Magi of the Orient appeared at the door ready to mount their camels.

"How beautiful and handsome they are!" said Carlos to the other stable boys as they held the camels for the Magi to mount.

Large parcels of food and pastries, jugs of water, and innumerable baskets full of all kinds of toys were brought out and tied tightly on the camels' backs. Then the Three Kings began their long journey.

On and on they went. As they entered the desert, night fell.

"Dark and somber indeed is the night," said King Gaspar.

"Fear not," remarked King Melchor, "the star will soon appear to guide us as it appears every year, the same star that led us twenty centuries ago to the stable at Bethlehem."

He had hardly finished talking when up above their heads appeared a strange star glittering in the dark.

"There is the star," said King Melchor.

"Seems to me," said King Baltazar, "that on our last journey the star always appeared much later; however, I may have lost all sense of time."

They followed the course it led. . . . On and on they went. For hours they traveled.

Suddenly, from behind a cloud a ray of light appeared and darkness gave way to daylight. The sun came out and the strange star disappeared.

Slowly the Three Magi pulled up their reins. "Alas," they exclaimed, "what is the meaning of this?" To their great surprise, after having ridden all night, they were standing at their very door—the door of their own castle.

"What can this mean?" asked King Gaspar.

"It means," answered King Melchor, "that in the course of the evening we have come back to our starting point."

"But we followed the star," said King Baltazar in a doleful voice.

"That was no star," piped a small voice.

"Wh-who speaks?" called out King Baltazar—this time in an excited voice.

"Oh, only me," said a little black beetle, coming out from one of the camel's ears.

"You!" cried King Melchor. "How do you know . . . ?"

"Tell us, little beetle, tell us all you know," said King Gaspar.

"The star," said the little beetle, trying to raise its voice loud enough for them to hear, "was just a number of fireflies in formation to imitate a star."

"What are we to do?" moaned King Melchor. "We will never reach Spain. *For the first time the children will find their shoes empty.* What are we to do?"

"Shush—" said the beetle. "Look!"

Running toward them so fast his thin legs scarcely touched the ground was a little gray mouse.

"Ratón Perez!" exclaimed the Kings.

"My Kings," said Ratón Perez, "it's all the horses' fault. They are very jealous. While they discussed their plans with the fireflies, I chanced to be resting on a bundle of straw. Too late to follow you, I thought of a plan to undo the fireflies' work. What could be easier than to ask Father Time? It was, as you know, a question of time and only he could arrange it. To my great surprise, I found Father Time sound asleep over his great clock. Not to cause him the least discomfort, lest I should wake him, I set his clock back twenty-four hours. So now, my good Magi, ride on! The children of Spain must have their toys."

As if led by an invisible hand, the three camels pricked up their ears, raised their heads, and went on toward the desert. Silence descended upon the group. Above them was the blue sky and all around them was the sand, hot like fire under the rays of the sun. The Magi looked at each other in silence and set their eyes on the road.

Darkness soon closed in. On and on the camels went. They could hardly see themselves in the darkness that enveloped them.

Suddenly a star appeared, large and resplendent, way up in the sky. Its light shone like a silver thread on the sand. In great silence, the Three Magi raised their heads to the sky and gazed long at the star. There was hope and faith in the three eager faces that now bent their heads to urge the camels on.

From somewhere a sound of bells was heard, faintly at first, then louder and louder.

"God be praised," said King Baltazar, "we are near the city. It's the tolling of the bells—the bells from the church tower, ringing as a reminder of the entrance of Joseph and Mary to Bethlehem years ago."

Ding—dong—ding—dong.

The bells chimed merrily now and the hour of twelve struck. The camels shook their heads, making all their headgear tinkle. Strangely enough, they picked up the tempo of the bells and almost in unison passed the opened gate into the city.

That morning under each bed, inside each shoe, beside baskets and boxes wrapped with straw and flowers, the children found their gifts, unaware of the hardships the Three Magi had had in keeping faith with them.

THERE WAS A SHIP A-SAILING

There was a ship a-sailing,
A-sailing on the sea.
And it was deeply laden,
With pretty things for me.

There were raisins in the cabin,
And almonds in the hold,
The sails were made of satin,
And the mast it was of gold.

The four-and-twenty sailors
That stood between the decks
Were four-and-twenty white mice
With rings about their necks.

The captain was a duck, a duck,
With a jacket on his back,
And when this fairy ship set sail,
The captain he said "Quack!"

ENGLISH SONG

Emmet Otter's Jug-Band Christmas

RUSSELL HOBAN

Christmas was coming and it was coming fast. It was coming to the river and the little run-down place where Emmet Otter and his mother lived, near Frogtown Hollow. Christmas was coming, and money was more scarce than ever.

Emmet Otter's father was dead, and his mother took in washing. Mrs. Otter did her washing with a washboard and a washtub, all by hand. Emmet hauled the water and he did the chores. He cut the firewood and he stacked it. He went out with the tool chest Pa had left him, and he did odd jobs around the neighborhood. Every day he went out fishing. So there was always something on the table, and between the two of them Emmet and his mother scraped along somehow.

But it was always hard going, and this year was harder than ever. The crops hadn't been good; the sawmill down the river had been slow, and many animals were out of work. "We'll get by somehow," Emmet and his mother used to say to each other. "We always have." But they were tired of just getting by.

"Last year I gave Emmet a muffler that I'd knitted," Mrs. Otter said to Irma Coon, "and the year before that it was mittens."

"Nothing wrong with mufflers and mittens, Alice," said Irma Coon. "It's the thought that counts."

"I know all about that," said Mrs. Otter. "But it's been such a rock-bottom life for so long, just once at least I'd like to bust out with a real glorious Christmas for Emmet—something shiny and expensive."

"It's a bad year for that," said Irma Coon.

"It's always a bad year," said Alice Otter, and she went on with her washing.

"Ma's never had it easy," Emmet said to Charlie Beaver. "We never had much even when Pa was alive, what with him being a traveling man, always up and down the river selling snake oil. Ma never complained, though. She said if Pa was willing to take a chance on snake oil, she was willing to take a chance on him. I wish I could fix it so she didn't have to do any more washing, and if I can't do that, at least I'd like to give her one real good Christmas.''

"There's no odd jobs this year," said Charlie. "I can't make a nickel. Maybe it'll be a better Christmas next year."

"Some year it's got to be this year," said Emmet. "Last year I made Ma a sewing box, and the year before I carved a pie-crimper. Sometime she's got to have something fine and fancy that costs money."

"Money's hard to come by," said Charlie, and he and Emmet both went off to do their chores.

In the evening Ma and Emmet read aloud to each other by candlelight the way they always did, but neither one was paying attention to the book. Ma was thinking about a present for Emmet and Emmet was thinking about a present for Ma.

After they finished reading, Ma and Emmet sang together. They sang *Down the Slide with Dora, Swimming Nellie Home, The Bathing Suit That Grandma Otter Wore, We'll Go Fishing in the Moonlight,* and ended up with their favorite hymn, *Downstream Where the River Meets the Sea.*

Mrs. Otter had a lovely voice, and Emmet remembered her telling him that she had played the piano when she was a girl. Emmet wondered how many odd jobs it would take to buy Ma a piano, and he knew that he would probably never in his life be able to save up that much money. But the idea of a piano stayed in his mind and kept on growing.

Ma was thinking too. She was remembering how Emmet had looked at a beautiful secondhand guitar with mother-of-pearl inlays in a store window in town. Ma thought about how many washes it would take to buy that guitar for Emmet. Ma wanted Emmet to have that guitar for Christmas, and she didn't know what she could do about it.

Christmas was just two weeks off when Ma and Emmet heard some news that interested them both.

"Fifty dollars cash," said Harvey Muskrat. "How's that for a prize?"

"Prize for what?" said Emmet.

"The Merchants' Association is putting on a talent show in Waterville," said Harvey.

"What kind of talent?" Emmet asked.

"Anything," said Harvey. "Singing, dancing, playing instruments, reciting, acrobatics, juggling—anything at all. Have you got any talent?"

"I don't know," said Emmet. "Have you?"

"I've got a kazoo," said Harvey. "Wendell Coon knows how to blow a jug. Charlie Beaver has a cigar-box banjo. We could have what they call a jug band, maybe. We could call it the Frogtown Hollow Jug Band. All we need is a washtub bass."

"A washtub bass," said Emmet.

"That's right," said Harvey. "You set a washtub upside down, stand a broom handle up on the rim, and run a string from the top of the broom handle down through a little hole in the center of the tub. Then you strum it like a regular bass fiddle."

"A little hole in the center of the tub," said Emmet. "The trouble is, once you make a hole in the tub it won't hold water any more."

"Fifty dollars cash," said Harvey. "You could buy a lot of new washtubs with your share."

Emmet thought about it. If the Frogtown Hollow Jug Band won the prize, his share would be twelve dollars and fifty cents. With that he could buy a new washtub for a dollar and a half, put eleven dollars down on a secondhand piano, and pay out the rest. "When is the talent show?" he asked Harvey.

"Two days before Christmas," said Harvey.

"I'll think about it," said Emmet, and he walked slowly home.

While Harvey was telling Emmet about the talent show, Harvey's mother was telling Emmet's mother. "I wish I had some talent," Hetty Muskrat said. "We sure could use that money."

"I guess we all could," Mrs. Otter said, wondering whether there would be any really good singers in the show.

That night at dinner Ma and Emmet could hardly look each other in the eye. When they took turns reading, they kept losing the place in the book, and when they got around to singing *Downstream Where the River Meets the Sea,* they both choked up a little.

The next morning at breakfast time the Otter house was empty. Ma's washtub was not in its regular place in the kitchen, and the broom was gone. Emmet's tool chest was not at the foot of the bed where he always kept it. There was a note on Emmet's pillow and there was a note on the kitchen table.

The note on Emmet's pillow said:

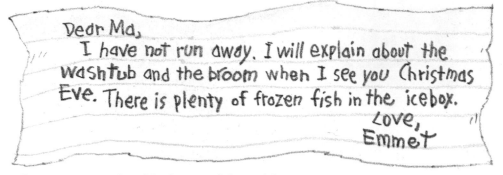

Dear Ma,
I have not run away. I will explain about the washtub and the broom when I see you Christmas Eve. There is plenty of frozen fish in the icebox.
Love,
Emmet

The note on the kitchen table said:

Dear Emmet,
I have not run away. I will explain about your tool chest when I see you Christmas Eve. There are clean underwear and shirts in your drawer.
Love,
Ma

Upriver, past Osprey Point, was a little hut that Emmet and his friends had built there for a clubhouse. In the hut Wendell Coon was blowing his jug; Harvey Muskrat was playing his kazoo; Charlie Beaver was picking his cigar-box banjo. And Emmet was strumming on his washtub bass and worrying.

Charlie Beaver was singing the words while he picked his banjo:

"Going to Old Man Possum's shack—
Sister Possum waiting out back."

But Emmet was singing under his breath:

"Can't pay the rent if Ma can't scrub,
Can't pay the rent with a hole in the tub."

"You better get with the beat, Emmet, if we're going to win," said Charlie.

Well, thought Emmet, if the Jug Band didn't win, maybe he and Ma could go away someplace where things were better. As long as he had his tool chest, he could do odd jobs and they would get along somehow. But Ma wasn't going to have a piano unless they won.

While the Frogtown Hollow Jug Band was practicing upriver, Ma was sitting at Esther Snapper's sewing machine, making herself a dress to wear at the talent show.

"I don't quite understand this whole thing, Alice," said Esther. "You pawned Emmet's tool chest so you could buy that dress material?"

"That's right," said Ma. "And I'm going to sing in the talent show, and if I win the fifty dollars, Emmet's going to have that guitar with the mother-of-pearl inlays."

"But what if you don't win?" said Esther.

"I've still got my washtub," said Ma, "and we can always move on to someplace where things are better. They surely couldn't be much worse."

"It sounds mighty chancy," said Esther, "but I certainly hope you win."

"Got to win," said Ma.

When the dress was finished, she practiced her songs in front of Esther's mirror and tried hard not to think of Emmet's tool chest that Pa had left him.

The night before Christmas Eve, the town hall in Waterville was all lit up for the talent show. Backstage the performers were getting ready to go on. Emmet was in the men's dressing room and Ma was in the ladies', so they did not see each other.

Everybody in the Frogtown Hollow Jug Band was nervous. "We've got a good band," said Wendell Coon.

"Got to win," said Emmet, and just as he said that, a whole lot of big cases on wheels rolled in with a whole lot of musicians following after.

"Who are you?" said Emmet.

One of the musicians, a woodchuck, pulled the cover off a set of drums. On the big drum was the name *The Nightmare.*

"We're from River Bend," said the woodchuck. "Pete Squirrel and Jimmy Possum on the electric guitar; Herman 'Fats' Porcupine on electric bass; Jethro, Gideon, and Amos Mouse on electric organ; Henry 'Jellohead' Woodchuck—that's me—on drums; Mary Jane Chipmunk doing the vocals; and Fred Rabbit working the lights."

"We might as well go home," said Harvey Muskrat.

"Too late to back out now," said Emmet, and he tried to think of ways to plug the hole in the washtub. Then it was time for the talent show to begin.

The first act was Steve and Selma Rabbit, who tap-danced. Then Bascom Crow recited a tragic poem. Bertha Toad and Winston Newt did a combination acrobatic and baton-twirling act. After each act the audience clapped a little and coughed a lot.

Then came the River Bend Nightmare, all of them wearing silvery, spangled costumes. They played a song called *Riverbottom Rock,* and while they played, the colored lights were making designs and patterns that jumped and shook and streaked like lightning on the walls and ceiling. The music roared and crashed and rattled windows all over town while Mary Jane Chipmunk moaned and hollered and screamed into the microphone.

When they were finished, the audience clapped and clapped for them to do an encore, and for their encore the River Bend Nightmare did *Swampland Stone.* The music roared and the lights flashed and the

windows rattled again. And when the clapping finally died down, the silence filled the town hall like water filling up a boat with a big hole in the bottom.

Ma sang her song next, and it was like a whisper far away that nobody could hear.

Then came the Frogtown Hollow Jug Band, and when Emmet and Harvey and Wendell and Charlie played their music, it didn't seem to make any more of a sound than crickets and night peepers.

Then there were a few more acts. Somebody juggled and somebody else did magic tricks. Then the judges gave the fifty-dollar cash prize to the River Bend Nightmare. Everybody wished everybody else a Merry Christmas and they all went home.

Ma and the Frogtown Hollow Jug Band were left by themselves standing in the street outside the town hall.

"Did you get my note?" said Ma to Emmet.

"No," said Emmet. "Did you get mine?"

"No," said Ma.

So they explained to each other about the washtub and the broom and the tool chest.

"Well," said Ma, "we took a chance and we lost. That's how it goes."

"That's how it goes," said Emmet.

"It isn't going to be much of a Christmas for us this year," said Ma. "I was hoping to get you that guitar you liked."

"I was thinking of a piano for you," said Emmet.

"I guess I ought to feel pretty bad," said Ma, "but the funny thing is that I don't. I feel pretty good."

"So do I," said Emmet. "I don't know why, but I do."

Harvey Muskrat took his kazoo out of his pocket and began to play *Sister Possum* softly as they walked.

"That's a nice little tune," said Ma. "How do the words go?"

Charlie Beaver sang them for her, then Ma sang:

> "Going to Old Man Possum's shack—
> Sister Possum waiting out back."

Then they all joined in the chorus:

> "Rowing on the river,
> Rowing on the water,
> Going to dance the whole night long
> With Old Man Possum's daughter."

"Let's try it with the whole band playing," said Ma. They were passing Doc Bullfrog's Riverside Rest and stopped by the boat landing. Up above them in the lighted windows they could see everyone having a good time and they could hear the clatter of dishes, the tinkle of glasses, and the sound of laughter.

Harvey played his kazoo, Wendell blew his jug, Charlie picked his cigar-box banjo, Emmet strummed his bass, and Ma sang as they all came on strong with *Sister Possum.* The music took off into the cold, clear air over the frozen river, and for a while they forgot the hard year they had had and the poor Christmas they could look forward to. Nobody noticed that the doors of the Riverside Rest had opened and Doc Bullfrog and his customers were listening.

"That's a mighty cheerful sound," said Doc Bullfrog. "What do you call your group?"

"Ma Otter and the Frogtown Hollow Boys," said Emmet.

"That's a good name too," said Doc Bullfrog. "How'd you like to play regular at the Riverside Rest?"

"Is the pay regular when you play regular?" said Emmet.

"It sure is," said Doc, "and your meals are on the house."

"What do you think, boys?" said Ma.

"We think we'd like that," said the boys.

"So would I," said Ma.

"Why not start tonight then?" said Doc Bullfrog. "After you have some dinner."

So they all went inside with Doc and had a good dinner. Then the band played and Ma sang until it was very late, and when they left for home they all had money in their pockets.

"Well," said Emmet to Ma, "it looks like I won't have to plug the hole in the washtub, and I won't have to buy you a new one either."

"We've still got to have clean clothes to wear," said Ma. "What am I going to wash them in?"

"From now on we're going to send our laundry out," said Emmet.

Ma was quiet for a few moments; then she said, "I think I'd like to do a song for Pa, right here and now. He took a chance on snake oil, and you took a chance on a washtub. He'd have been proud of us tonight."

So Ma Otter and the Frogtown Hollow Boys stopped there on the ice at three o'clock in the morning of Christmas Eve, and they did *Downstream Where the River Meets the Sea* for Pa.

Christmas Carol

The Kings they came from out the South,
    All dressed in ermine fine:
They bore Him gold and chrysoprase,
    And gifts of precious wine.

The Shepherds came from out the North,
    Their coats were brown and old:
They brought Him little newborn lambs—
    They had not any gold.

The Wise Men came from out the East,
    And they were wrapped in white:
The star that led them all the way
    Did glorify the night.

The Angels came from heaven high,
    And they were clad with wings:
And lo they brought a joyful song
    The host of heaven sings.

The Kings they knocked upon the door,
    The Wise Men entered in,
The Shepherds followed after them
    To hear the song begin.

The Angels sang through all the night
    Until the rising sun,
But little Jesus fell asleep
    Before the song was done.

SARA TEASDALE

SHEPHERD'S SONG AT CHRISTMAS

Look there at the star!
I, among the least,
Will arise and take
A journey to the East.
But what shall I bring
As a present for the King?
What shall I bring to the Manger?

    I will bring a song,
    A song that I will sing,
    In the Manger.

Watch out for my flocks,
Do not let them stray.
I am going on a journey
Far, far away.
But what shall I bring
As a present for the Child?
What shall I bring to the Manger?

    I will bring a lamb,
    Gentle, meek, and mild,
    A lamb for the Child
    In the Manger.

LANGSTON HUGHES

HOW WE MADE CHRISTMAS

GREY OWL

I arrived home in the thick of the blizzard and found the little cabin mighty snug to come into. Anahareo had busied herself crocheting bright wool borders on white sugar bags, split open and freshly laundered, and we now had these for window curtains, which gave everything a real cozy, homey appearance.

Our pet beavers, McGinnis and McGinty, had missed me. McGinnis especially had seemed to search for something, and had spent much time at the door, looking up at it. Neither of them was in view, but a nose was visible at the peephole, and finally being satisfied as to my identity, they came bouncing out and capered around me. McGinnis repeatedly threw himself at my feet until I offered both of them sticks of candy, which they sat and ate with loud and unmannerly sounds of satisfaction.

I laid out my small purchases which the kindly storekeeper had suggested that I make, saying as he did so that it must be lonesome in the woods and that he liked to feel that we would be having a Christmas celebration. So now that we had settled in Quebec, where Christmas was a real festival, we decided that we ought to make all the good cheer we could.

I whittled out some boards of dry cedar, painted them with Indian designs, and attached them to the sides and tops of the windows, where they looked, if not too closely inspected, like plaques of beadwork. We painted hanging ornaments with tribal emblems and hung them in places where the light fell on them. We laid two rugs of deerskin; these were immediately seized as toys by the two Macs and had to be nailed down. I made a warbonnet, a brave affair of paint and eagle feathers and imitation beadwork that sat on a wooden block carved to look like a warrior's face, and painted with the Friendship Sign in case we had a guest. We distributed colored candles in promi-

nent places and hung a Japanese lantern from the rafter. Viewed from the outside, through a window, the interior exhibited a very pleasing appearance.

On Christmas Eve all was ready. But there was one thing missing: Anahareo decided that the beavers were to have a Christmas tree. So while I lit the lantern and arranged the candles so their light fell on the decorations, and put apples and oranges and nuts in dishes on the table, and tended the saddle of deer meat that sizzled alongside the factory-made Christmas pudding that was boiling on top of the little stove, Anahareo took an axe and snowshoes and went out into the starry Christmas night.

After a brief trudge in the snow, she found a fine balsam fir, a very picture of a Christmas tree, which she wedged upright in a crevice in the floor poles. On top of it she put a lighted candle, and on the limbs tied candies and pieces of apple and small delicacies from the table, so they hung there by strings and could be reached.

The beavers viewed these preparations with no particular enthusiasm, but before long, attracted by the odor of the tree, they found the hanging tidbits and sampled them. Soon they were busy cutting the strings and pulling them down and eating with great gusto. And we set our own feast on the table, and as we ate we watched them. They soon ate all there was on the tree, and as these were replaced the little creatures stood up on their hind legs and grabbed and pulled at their presents and stole choice morsels from one another. They pushed and shoved so that they would sometimes fall and scramble to their feet again as hastily as possible, for fear everything would be gone before they got up. They screeched and chattered and squealed in their excitement, and we forgot our supper and laughed and called out at them, and they ran to us excitedly and back to the tree with little squawks as if to say "Looky what we found!"

And when they could eat no more, they began to carry away provisions, sometimes between their teeth, on all fours, or staggering along erect with some prized tidbit clutched tightly in their arms, each apparently bent on getting all that could be got while it lasted. And when we thought they had enough and no longer made replacements, McGinty, the wise and the thrifty, pulled down the tree and started away with it, as though she figured on another crop appearing later.

It was the best fun of the evening, and instead of us making a festival for them, they made one for us and provided us with a Christmas entertainment such as had never before been seen in any other home, I'm pretty sure, or anywhere in all the province of Quebec.

THE TWELVE DAYS OF CHRISTMAS

On the first day of Christmas
My true love sent to me
A partridge in a pear tree.

On the second day of Christmas
My true love sent to me
Two turtledoves
And a partridge in a pear tree.

On the third day of Christmas
My true love sent to me
Three French hens,
Two turtledoves,
And a partridge in a pear tree.

On the fourth day of Christmas
My true love sent to me
Four calling birds,
Three French hens,
Two turtledoves,
And a partridge in a pear tree.

On the fifth day of Christmas
My true love sent to me
Five gold rings,
Four calling birds,
Three French hens,
Two turtledoves,
And a partridge in a pear tree.

On the sixth day of Christmas
My true love sent to me
Six geese a-laying,
Five gold rings,
Four calling birds,
Three French hens,
Two turtledoves,
And a partridge in a pear tree.

On the seventh day of Christmas
My true love sent to me
Seven swans a-swimming,
Six geese a-laying,
Five gold rings,
Four calling birds,
Three French hens,
Two turtledoves,
And a partridge in a pear tree.

On the eighth day of Christmas
My true love sent to me
Eight maids a-milking,
Seven swans a-swimming,
Six geese a-laying,
Five gold rings,
Four calling birds,
Three French hens,
Two turtledoves,
And a partridge in a pear tree.

On the ninth day of Christmas
My true love sent to me
Nine drummers drumming,
Eight maids a-milking,
Seven swans a-swimming,
Six geese a-laying,
Five gold rings,
Four calling birds,
Three French hens,
Two turtledoves,
And a partridge in a pear tree.

On the tenth day of Christmas
My true love sent to me
Ten pipers piping,
Nine drummers drumming,
Eight maids a-milking,
Seven swans a-swimming,
Six geese a-laying,
Five gold rings,
Four calling birds,
Three French hens,
Two turtledoves,
And a partridge in a pear tree.

On the eleventh day of Christmas
My true love sent to me
Eleven ladies dancing,
Ten pipers piping,
Nine drummers drumming,
Eight maids a-milking,
Seven swans a-swimming,
Six geese a-laying,
Five gold rings,
Four calling birds,
Three French hens,
Two turtledoves,
And a partridge in a pear tree.

On the twelfth day of Christmas
My true love sent to me
Twelve lords a-leaping,
Eleven ladies dancing,
Ten pipers piping,
Nine drummers drumming,
Eight maids a-milking,
Seven swans a-swimming,
Six geese a-laying,
Five gold rings,
Four calling birds,
Three French hens,
Two turtledoves,
And a partridge in a pear tree.

TRADITIONAL

A MERRY LITERARY CHRISTMAS

When Christmas shopping time
   draws nigh,
And I am faced with gifts to buy,
I think about one relative
Who always had one gift to give.
Year after year her present came,
And every year it was the same.
While other gifts were round and fat,
(Their secrets hidden) hers was flat,
Rectangular, the corners square,
I knew exactly what was there.
I'd pass it by without a look—
My aunt had sent another book!
I'd only open it to write
A "thank-you" that was too polite,
But every year when Christmas went
I'd read the book my aunt had sent,
And looking back, I realize
Each gift was treasure in disguise.
So now it's time to write her here
A thank-you note that is sincere.

So—thanks for Alice and Sara Crewe,
For Christopher Robin and Piglet and Pooh,
For Little Nell and William Tell
And Peter and Wendy and Tinker Bell.

Thanks for Tom and Jim and Huck,
For Robinson Crusoe and Dab-Dab the duck,
For Meg and Jo and Johnny Crow
And Papa Geppetto's Pinocchio.

For Mary Poppins and Rat and Toad,
King Arthur and Dorothy's Yellow Brick Road,
For Kipling's Kim and tales from Grimm,
And Ferdinand, Babar, and Tiny Tim.

I loved them all, I'm glad I met them.
They're with me still, I won't forget them.
So I'll give books on Christmas Day
Though I know what all my nieces say—
I know it from the way they write
A "thank-you" that is too polite.

ALICE LOW

CHRISTMAS EVERY DAY

ABRIDGED AND ADAPTED FROM THE STORY BY WILLIAM DEAN HOWELLS

Once there was a little girl who liked Christmas so much that she wanted it to be Christmas every day in the year, and as soon as Thanksgiving was over she began to send postal cards to the old Christmas Fairy to ask if she mightn't have it. But the old fairy never answered any of the postals, and after a while the little girl found out that the fairy was pretty particular and wouldn't even notice anything but real letters on sheets of paper, and sealed outside with a mono-gram—or your initial, anyway. So then she began to send her letters; and in about three weeks—or just the day before Christmas, it was— she got a letter from the fairy saying she might have it Christmas every day for a year, and then they would see about having it longer.

The little girl was a good deal excited already, preparing for the old-fashioned, once-a-year Christmas that was coming the next day, and perhaps the fairy's promise didn't make such an impression on her as it would have made at some other time. She just resolved to keep it to herself, and surprise everybody with it as it kept coming true; and then it slipped out of her mind altogether.

She had a splendid Christmas. She went to bed early, so as to let Santa Claus have a chance at the stockings, and in the morning she was up the first of anybody and went and felt them, and found hers all lumpy with packages of candy, and oranges and grapes, and pock-etbooks and rubber balls, and all kinds of small presents, just as they always had every Christmas. Then she waited around until the rest of the family were up, and she was the first to burst into the library, when the doors were opened, and look at the large presents laid out on the library table—books and portfolios and boxes of stationery, and dolls and little stoves, and dozens of handkerchiefs, and inkstands and skates and snow shovels and photograph frames, and little easels and boxes of watercolors and candied cherries and dolls' houses, and

waterproofs—and the big Christmas tree, lighted and standing in a wastebasket in the middle.

She had a splendid Christmas all day. She ate so much candy that she did not want any breakfast; and the whole forenoon the presents kept pouring in, and she went around giving the presents she had got for other people, and came home and ate turkey and cranberry for dinner, and plum pudding and nuts and raisins and oranges and more candy, and then went out and coasted and came in with a stomach-ache, crying, and they had a light supper, and pretty early everybody went to bed cross.

The little girl slept very heavily, and she slept very late, but she was wakened at last by the other children dancing around her bed with their stockings full of presents in their hands.

"What is it?" said the little girl, and she rubbed her eyes and tried to rise up in bed.

"Christmas! Christmas! Christmas!" they all shouted, and waved their stockings.

"Nonsense! It was Christmas yesterday."

Her brothers and sisters just laughed. "We don't know about that. It's Christmas today, anyway. You come into the library and see."

Then all at once it flashed on the little girl that the fairy was keeping her promise, and her year of Christmases was beginning. She was dreadfully sleepy, but she sprang up like a lark—a lark that had overeaten itself and gone to bed cross—and darted into the library. There it was again! Books and portfolios and boxes of stationery and the Christmas tree blazing away, and the family picking out their presents, but looking pretty sleepy, and her father perfectly puzzled, and her mother ready to cry. "I'm sure I don't see how I'm to dispose of all these things," said her mother, and her father said it seemed to him they had had something just like it the day before, but he supposed he must have dreamed it.

Well, the next day it was just the same thing over again, but everybody getting crosser; and at the end of a week's time so many people had lost their tempers that you could pick up lost tempers everywhere; they perfectly strewed the ground. Even when people tried to recover their tempers they usually got somebody else's, and it made the most dreadful mix.

The little girl began to get frightened, keeping the secret all to herself. She wanted to tell her mother, but she didn't dare to; and she was ashamed to ask the fairy to take back her gift, it seemed ungrateful and ill-bred, and she thought she would try to stand it, but she hardly knew how she could, for a whole year. So it went on and on, and it was Christmas on St. Valentine's Day and Washington's Birthday just the same as any day.

After a while, turkeys became so scarce they got to be about a thousand dollars apiece, and they got to passing off almost anything for turkeys. And cranberries—well, they asked a diamond apiece for cranberries. All the woods and orchards were cut down for Christmas trees, and where the woods and orchards used to be, it looked just like a stubble-field, with the stumps. After a while they had to make Christmas trees out of rags and stuff them with bran, like old-fashioned dolls; but there were plenty of rags, because people got so poor buying presents for one another that they couldn't get any new clothes, and they just wore their old ones to tatters.

Well, after it had gone on about three or four months the little girl, whenever she came into the room in the morning and saw those great ugly lumpy stockings dangling at the fireplace, and the disgusting presents around everywhere, used to just sit down and burst out crying. In six months she was perfectly exhausted; she couldn't even

cry anymore; she just lay on the lounge and rolled her eyes and panted. About the beginning of October she took to sitting down on dolls wherever she found them—French dolls, or any kind—she hated the sight of them so; and by Thanksgiving she was crazy and just slammed her presents across the room.

By that time people didn't carry presents around nicely anymore. They flung them over the fence, or through the window, or anything, and instead of taking great pains to write FOR DEAR PAPA or MAMA or BROTHER or SISTER or SUSIE or SAMMIE or BILLIE or BOBBY or JIMMIE or JENNIE, or whoever it was, and troubling to get the spelling right, and then signing their names and XMAS, 188—, they used to write in the gift books, TAKE IT, YOU HORRID OLD THING! and then go and bang it against the front door. Nearly everybody had built barns to hold their presents, but pretty soon the barns overflowed, and then they used to let the presents lie out in the rain, or anywhere. Sometimes the police used to come and tell them to shovel their presents off the sidewalk, or they would arrest them.

Well, before it came Thanksgiving, it had leaked out who had caused all these Christmases. The little girl had suffered so much that she had talked about it in her sleep, and after that, hardly anybody would play with her. People just perfectly despised her, because if it had not been for her greediness, it wouldn't have happened. So now, when it came Thanksgiving, and she wanted them to go to church, and have a squash pie and turkey, and show their gratitude, they said that all the turkeys had been eaten up for her old Christmas dinners, and if she would stop the Christmases, they would see about the gratitude. The very next day the little girl began to send letters to the Christmas Fairy, and then telegrams, to stop it. But it didn't do any good; and then she got to calling at the fairy's house, but the girl that came to the door always said "Not at home," or "Engaged," or "At dinner," or something like that; and so it went on until it came to the old once-a-year Christmas Eve. The little girl fell asleep, and when she woke up in the morning—it wasn't Christmas.

Well, there was the greatest rejoicing all over the country, and it extended clear up into Canada. The people met together everywhere, and kissed and cried for joy. The city carts went around and gathered

up all the candy and raisins and nuts and dumped them into the river; and it made the fish perfectly sick; and the whole United States, as far out as Alaska, was one blaze of bonfires, where the children were burning up their gift books and presents of all kinds. They had the greatest *time*!

The little girl went to thank the old fairy because she had stopped it being Christmas, and she said she hoped she would keep her promise and see that Christmas never, never came again. Then the fairy frowned and asked her if she was sure she knew what she meant. And the little girl asked her, Why not? And the old fairy said that now she was behaving just as greedily as ever, and she'd better look out. This made the little girl think it all over carefully again, and she said she would be willing to have it Christmas about once in a thousand years; and then she said a hundred, and then she said ten, and at last she got down to one. Then the fairy said that was the good old way that had pleased people ever since Christmas began, and she was agreed. Then the little girl said, "What're your shoes made of?" And the fairy said, "Leather." And the little girl said, "Bargain's done forever," and skipped off, and hippity-hopped the whole way home, she was so glad.

AN OLD CHRISTMAS GREETING

Sing Hey! Sing Hey!
For Christmas Day,
Twine mistletoe and holly;
For friendship grows
In winter snows,
And so let's all be jolly.

ANONYMOUS

MERRY CHRISTMAS

M for the **M**usic, merry and clear;
E for the **E**ve, the crown of the year;
R for the **R**omping of bright girls and boys;
R for the **R**eindeer that bring them the toys;
Y for the **Y**ule log softly aglow.

C for the **C**old of the sky and the snow;
H for the **H**earth where they hang up the hose;
R for the **R**eel which the old folks propose;
I for the **I**cicles seen through the pane;
S for the **S**leigh bells, with tinkling refrain;
T for the **T**ree with gifts all abloom;
M for the **M**istletoe hung in the room;
A for the **A**nthems we all love to hear;
S for **S**t. Nicholas—joy of the year!

FROM *ST. NICHOLAS* MAGAZINE, JANUARY 1897

CHRISTMAS EVE

My stocking's where
He'll see it—there!
One-half a pair.

The tree is sprayed,
My prayers are prayed,
My wants are weighed.

I've made a list
Of what he missed
Last year. I've kissed

My father, mother,
Sister, brother;
I've done those other

Things I should
And would and could.
So far, so good.

DAVID MCCORD

COBWEB CHRISTMAS

SHIRLEY CLIMO

Once upon a Christmastime, long ago in Germany, there lived a little old woman. She was so little she had to climb upon a step stool to reach her feather bed and so old she couldn't even count all the Christmases she'd seen. The children in her village called her Tante, which means "Auntie" in German.

Tante's home was a cottage at the edge of a thick fir forest. The cottage had but one room, one door, and one window, and no upstairs to it at all. It suited the old woman, for there was room enough within its walls for her to keep a canary for singing, a cat for purring, and a dog to doze beside the fire.

Squeezed up against the cottage was a barn. The barn was a bit bigger, and in it Tante kept a donkey for riding, and a cow and a goat for milk and cheese. She had a noisy rooster as well to crow her out of bed each morning, and a speckled hen to lay an egg for her breakfast. With so many animals about, the tiny cottage wasn't tidy, but Tante didn't fuss over a few feathers, a little fur, or a spiderweb or two.

Except once a year, when the days got short and the nights grew long the old woman would nod her head and say, "Time to clean for Christmas."

Then she'd shake the quilt and wash the window and scour the soot from the kettle. She'd scrub the floor on her hands and knees and stand tiptoe on her step stool to sweep the cobwebs from the ceiling.

This Christmas was just as always.

"Wake up!" said Tante, snapping her fingers. The dog stopped dreaming and dashed off to dig for bones beneath the bushes.

"Scat!" cried Tante, flapping her apron. The cat hid under the bedclothes and the canary flew to the chimney top.

"Shoo!" scolded Tante, swishing her broom. All the spiders and each little wisp of web went flying out the door as well.

When she'd washed and wiped every crack and corner of the cottage, the old woman nodded her head and said, "Time to fetch Christmas."

Then Tante took the axe from its peg in the barn and hung the harness with the bells upon the donkey. She scrambled onto the donkey's back, nimble as a mouse, and the two jogged and jingled into the fir forest. They circled all around, looking for a tree to fit Tante's liking.

"Too big!" said she of some, and "Crooked as a pretzel!" of others.

At last she spied a fir that grew straight, but not tall, bushy, but not wide. When the wind blew, the tree bent and bobbed a curtsey to the little old woman.

"It wants to come for Christmas," Tante told the donkey, "and so it shall."

She chopped down the tree with her axe, taking care to leave a bough or two so it might grow again. And they went home, only now the donkey trotted with the tree upon his back and the old lady skipped along beside.

The tree fit the cottage as snugly as if it had sprouted there. The top touched the rafters, and the tips of the branches brushed the window on one side and the door frame on the other. The old woman nodded her head and said, "Time to make Christmas."

Then Tante made cookies. She made gingerbread boys and girls. She baked almond cookies, cut into crescents like new moons, and cinnamon cookies, shaped like stars. When she'd sprinkled them with sugar and hung them on the tree, they looked as if they'd fallen straight from the frosty sky. Next she rubbed apples until they gleamed like glass and hung these up, too. Tante put a red ribbon on a bone for the dog and tied up a sprig of catnip for the cat. She stuck bites of cheese into pinecones for the mice and bundled bits of oats to tuck among the branches for the donkey and the cow and the goat. She strung nuts for the squirrels, wove garlands of seeds for the birds, and cracked corn into a basket for the chickens. There was something for everyone on Tante's tree, except, of course, for the spiders, for they'd been brushed away.

When she was done, the old woman nodded her head and said, "Time to share Christmas."

Tante invited all the children in the village to come and see the tree, as she did every year.

"Tante!" the children cried, "that's the most wonderful tree in the world!"

When the children had nibbled the apples and sampled the cookies, they went home to their beds to wait for Christkindel. Christkindel was the spirit who went from house to house on Christmas Eve and slipped presents into the toes of their shoes.

Then the old woman invited the animals to come and share Christmas.

The dog and the cat and the canary and the chickens and some small shy wild creatures crowded into the cottage. The donkey and the cow and the goat peered in the window and steamed the pane with their warm breath. To each and every visitor, Tante gave a gift.

But no one could give Tante what she wanted. All of her life the little old woman had heard stories about marvelous happenings on Christmas Eve. Cocks would crow at midnight. Bees could hum a carol. Animals might speak aloud. More than anything else, Tante wanted some Christmas magic that was not of her own making. So the old woman sat down in her rocking chair and said, "Now it's time to wait for Christmas."

She nodded and nodded and nodded her head.

Tante was tired from the cleaning and the chopping and the cooking, and she fell fast asleep. If the rooster crowed when the clock struck twelve, Tante wasn't listening. She didn't hear if the donkey whispered in the cow's ear, or see if the dog danced jigs with the cat. The old woman snored in her chair, just as always.

She never heard the rusty, squeaky voices calling at her door, "Let us in!"

Someone else heard.

Christkindel was passing the cottage on his way to take the toys to the village children. He listened. He looked and saw hundreds of spiders sitting on Tante's doorstep.

"We've never had a Christmas," said the biggest spider. "We're always swept away. Please, Christkindel, may we peek at Tante's tree?"

So Christkindel opened the cottage door a crack, just wide enough to let a little starlight in. For what harm could come from looking?

And he let the spiders in as well.

Huge spiders, tiny spiders, smooth spiders, hairy spiders, spotted spiders, striped spiders, brown and black and yellow spiders, and the palest kind of see-through spiders came

creeping, crawling, sneaking softly,

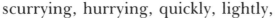

scurrying, hurrying, quickly, lightly,

zigging, zagging,
weaving, and wobbling
into the old woman's cottage.

The curious spiders crept closer and closer to the tree. One, two, three skittered up the trunk. All the other spiders followed the leaders.

They ran from branch to branch, in and out, back and forth, up and down the tree. Wherever the spiders went, they left a trail behind. Threads looped from limb to limb, and webs were woven everywhere.

Now the spiders weren't curious any longer. They'd seen Christmas. They'd felt Christmas, every twig on the tree, so they scuttled away.

When Christkindel came back to latch the door he found Tante's tree tangled with sticky, stringy spiderwebs. He knew how hard the old woman had worked to clean her cottage. He understood how dismayed she'd be on Christmas morning. But he didn't blame the busy spiders. Instead he changed their cobwebs into a gift for Tante.

Christkindel touched the spokes of each web with his finger. The twisted strands turned shiny gold; the dangling threads sparkled like silver. Now the old woman's Christmas tree was truly the most wonderful in the world.

The rooster woke Tante in the morning.

"What's this?" cried Tante. She rubbed her eyes and blinked at the glittering tree. "Something marvelous has happened!"

Tante was puzzled, as well as pleased. So she climbed on her stool, the better to see how such magic was spun. At the tip top of the tree, one teeny, tiny spider, unnoticed by Christkindel, was finishing its web.

"Now I know why this Christmas is not like any other," said Tante.

The little old woman knew, too, that such miracles come but once. So, each Christmastime thereafter, she did not clean so carefully, but left a few webs in the rafters, so that the spiders might share Christmas. And every year, after she'd hung the cookies and the apples and the garlands on her tree, the little old woman would nod her head and say, "Time for Christmas magic."

Then Tante would weave tinsel among the branches, until the tree sparkled with strings of gold and silver. Just as her tree did on the Cobweb Christmas.

Just as Christmas trees do today.

THE JOY OF GIVING

Somehow, not only for Christmas
   But all the long year through,
The joy that you give to others
   Is the joy that comes back to you;
And the more you spend in blessing
   The poor and lonely and sad,
The more of your heart's possessing
   Returns to make you glad.

JOHN GREENLEAF WHITTIER

132

ACKNOWLEDGMENTS

134

ALICE LOW

has written stories, poems, and songs since she was a young girl. She is the former editor of the Children's Choice Book Club, has reviewed children's books for the *New York Times Book Review,* and is the author of more than fifteen books for young readers.

A mother and grandmother, Ms. Low lives in Briarcliff Manor, New York.

MARC BROWN

is the creator of many books for children, including the popular Arthur Adventure series. He has also illustrated the best-selling *Read-Aloud Rhymes for the Very Young* and collected and illustrated three books of verse: *Finger Rhymes, Hand Rhymes,* and *Party Rhymes.* His work has been widely praised for its warmth, whimsy, humor, and surefire appeal to children of all ages.

Mr. Brown lives with his wife, Laurie, and three children, Tolon, Tucker, and Eliza, in Hingham, Massachusetts.